# SWEETS

## Connie Shelton

# SECRET SWEETS

Samantha Sweet Mysteries, Book 18

## Connie Shelton

Secret Staircase Books

Secret Sweets
Published by Secret Staircase Books, an imprint of
Columbine Publishing Group, LLC
PO Box 416, Angel Fire, NM 87710

Book layout and design by Secret Staircase Books
Cover images © Makeitdoubleplz, BooksRMe, RKasprzak

First trade paperback edition: July, 2024
First e-book edition: July, 2024

\* \* \*

**Publisher's Cataloging-in-Publication Data**

Shelton, Connie
Secret Sweets / by Connie Shelton.
p. cm.
ISBN 978-1649141835 (paperback)
ISBN 978-1649141842 (e-book)

1. Samantha Sweet (Fictitious character)--Fiction. 2. Taos, New
Mexico—Fiction. 3. Paranormal activity—Fiction. 4. Bakery—
Fiction. 5. Women sleuths—Fiction. I. Title

Samantha Sweet Mystery Series : Book 18.
Shelton, Connie, Samantha Sweet mysteries.

BISAC : FICTION / Mystery & Detective.

813/.54

*For Dan, my partner in all things,*
*and Daisy who completes our pack.*

## Acknowledgements

The first few months of this year were difficult, personally, and I am ever grateful to all the readers who reached out to me with messages of comfort and love when my mother passed. Your support means so much to me. And to those supportive family members who helped ease the way through the loss of both parents—you know who you are. Love you!

On the publishing side of things, my books are always infinitely better for the editing and proofreading of my fabulous team. Stephanie Dewey, who always edits with love, Marcia Koopmann, Susan Gross, Eve Osborne, Sandra Anderson, Paula Webb, and Isobel Tamney—you ladies are the best at spotting the things that get past me. Thank you so very much!

# Chapter 1

Samantha Sweet wiped a smear of chocolate from her face and stared at the racks of autumn colors. Sugar cookies glazed in shades of red and orange, brownies with chocolate frosting and tiny fall leaves on them, miniature pecan pies. The Halloween rush was over, and Thanksgiving was nearly three weeks away. Julio, her head baker, had taken his annual motorcycle run through Colorado and Wyoming and returned this morning. Becky's kids were in school, and Jen—the girl who never took time off—swore she wouldn't need a break until after Christmas.

Sam felt this was the perfect time of year. Cool weather, brilliant autumn foliage, sunny days in which to relax, nights where a fire felt really good. She'd just begun to clear the mixing bowls and baking sheets from the worktable when the back door eased open and she spotted her daughter.

"I've got Ranger and Nellie ready to go," Kelly said. "All clean and fresh. Shall I put them in your truck, or would you rather we find them a kennel to wait in?"

"I'm just about done for the day." Sam smiled and carried the utensils to the sink where Julio already had soapy water waiting. "I'll meet you outside."

"Go ahead," Becky told her. "I'll get these goodies out to the display case so Jen will be ready for the after-school crowd."

"What about any custom orders?"

"There are two birthday cakes due tomorrow, plus the book club's chocolate—whatever you'd planned on."

"Yeah, gotta give that some thought." Sam pulled off her baker's jacket and picked up her bag. "Hopefully I'll have some brilliant inspiration by morning."

"Hey, if not, I can hold back a tray of these brownies. Never knew that group to turn down a fabulous brownie." Becky winked as she set a plastic cover over the pastries.

Sam called out a goodbye to Jen in the sales room, then walked out to her truck. There stood Kelly with their black Lab and border collie on leashes. Sam opened the back door and the dogs hopped up, one at a time.

"Something the matter?" Sam asked, eyeing the frown-wrinkles on her daughter's forehead. "Ana's okay, isn't she?"

"Oh yeah. She's talked her daddy into taking their science lesson into the woods today." Kelly shrugged. "Nah, it's just that Riki's been in a real mood all day. Nothing over there has gone right."

Sam glanced toward the back door of Puppy Chic, the grooming salon where one of Kelly's close friends had created a hugely successful business. "Super busy?"

"Not that so much. I dunno. She's got something else going on. I'll just shampoo dogs and keep my head down until it blows over." Kelly stepped in and gave Sam a hug. "It will. You know Riki. She's usually the picture of good cheer."

True. Their British transplant friend always seemed to love life here in Taos, and rarely complained about anything.

"Okay then. I'll take these two home and try to get them not to follow Beau out to the muddy side of the pasture again right away."

Kelly laughed and gave each of the dogs a little tickle on the ears through the truck's open window. "Talk soon, Mom."

Sam drove past the Plaza traffic, heading north from the center of town, noticing and appreciating the changing leaves. Soon, they would fade to brown before snow fell and provided a white vista for the winter months. She steered through the stone entry to the ranch, down the long driveway toward their log home, the dogs wriggling with excitement.

Beau's pickup was in its usual spot and she pulled her truck in beside his; the dogs ran to the front door the moment she let them out. When she opened the door, the heavenly scent of her husband's special chile con carne drifted out. She took a deep breath.

The dogs wasted no time in racing to the kitchen, where Beau stood at the stove, stirring the contents of the large stew pot, adjusting the temperature a little. Sam turned to hang her jacket on the wooden coat rack by the front door, noticing the fire that crackled in the stone fireplace. The last of the afternoon sun rays gleamed through the south-facing French doors and shone on the pine floor.

"Getting an early start on winter?" she teased as she

walked into the kitchen and slipped an arm around his waist.

He sent a crooked little smile her way. "Eh, yeah, I guess. I put the chile on early, the horses are already tended to, and you have to admit there's a nip in the air. Supposed to be in the twenties tonight."

"It's as good a reason as any I can think of." She stepped over and opened an upper cupboard. "Shall I set the table, or would you like to relax with a drink before we eat?"

"Either. You choose."

She pulled out his favorite beer stein and a wine glass for herself. Beau set the lid on the kettle and poured the drinks, which they carried to the living room. They stood at the back doors, clinking their glasses, and enjoying the wide open view of the ranch. Outside, the two horses grazed near a narrow stream that cut a gentle path through the property.

The electronic ring from the landline phone startled them both. No one ever called on that one, and they'd often discussed dropping the expense of it. Beau walked over to the cabinet where it sat and glanced at the caller ID.

"It's showing my hometown area code and prefix," he mumbled, reaching for the handset, automatically hitting the speaker button as he answered.

"Beau, it's Cecelia," came a voice through the line. "I need your help."

"Cece? What on earth?" He sent a puzzled look toward Sam.

"It's about Mark," she continued, desperation seeping into her tone. "He's … he was murdered, Beau. You're in law enforcement, and you're away from this town. I don't know who else to turn to."

# Chapter 2

Sam saw it in his face, the old thrill of a case calling out to him. For two years now, he'd said he wanted no part of his old job, that being a rancher was everything to him. But now his expression told a different story. She slipped upstairs to change out of her bakery clothing, leaving him to take the call in private.

"All right, Cecelia," Beau was saying, his voice steady as Sam closed their bedroom door. "I'm listening."

When she returned, ten minutes later, he'd set the phone down and was back in the kitchen.

"You okay, hon?" Samantha's voice floated from the doorway, warm and gentle.

"That was my cousin Cecelia," Beau muttered, stirring the pot mechanically, his expression showing that he was processing something completely unexpected.

Sam moved into the room. "She said something about Mark being murdered? Who's Mark?"

"Her husband. Cece is a little younger than me, couple years, I guess. We all grew up in the same neighborhood in Creston, Oklahoma. Her dad was my dad's brother. Up until my family moved to New Mexico, we attended the same school, went to the same church, practically did everything together."

She laid a comforting hand on his shoulder, a silent nudge to share more. "And Mark? Did you know him too?"

"Yeah. He was in my classes. We weren't close-close, if you know what I mean. I had ranch chores every minute I wasn't in school, and I think he played football. I didn't have time to follow that much."

"So, they were high school sweethearts," Sam mused.

"Uh-huh. Dad and Mama and I, we'd moved away by then, but we kept up with the rest of the Cardwells, until Daddy died."

"Why do you think she called you?"

"Did you hear the part where she mentioned my law enforcement experience? I think she thinks I'm still sheriff here, that I can magically look into some database and find answers for her." He ran a hand through his hair. "I just reckon she's scared, Sam." Beau's gaze was distant, focused on something in a distant past.

"Sounds like she needs you, Beau." Samantha's voice was soft but firm, a gentle prod toward action.

"Thing is," he sighed, "I haven't seen Cecelia in years. We … drifted, after that mess with Uncle Ray's will. She never did forgive me for taking sides."

"Okay, I'll have to hear that story some day. But family's family, Beau. There will always be a connection, and sometimes, they're the only ones you've got. You should go there, try to help."

"I guess you're right. Can't let the past get in the way of doing what's needed." A new resolve flickered in Beau's eyes, the spark reigniting his sense of purpose. "You're coming too. Well, if you want to and can get away."

Sam's bakery duties buzzed through her mind. It wasn't as if a business owner could just take off on a whim. Mechanically, she reached into the cupboard for their favorite chile bowls, while Beau stirred up a quick cornbread mix and put the muffins into the oven. While the cornbread baked, she made some calls, catching Jen as she was locking up Sweet's Sweets for the night and Becky at home. Both of them assured her they could manage fine. The next couple of weeks would be slow, and even with the need for dozens of Thanksgiving pies before the end of the month, Julio had the recipes down pat.

"Go," Becky repeated. "You and Beau can use some time away together, and he'll have fun reconnecting with his cousins."

Sam doubted that *fun* was on the agenda, but she let Becky stay with that impression.

When she called Kelly, she was more forthcoming with the reason for the trip, but even her daughter assured her that everything at home would be fine. "I can even figure out how to feed and groom the horses if you need me to come by your place while you're gone."

"Well, at least you're off the hook for that—Danny's here, and I'm sure Beau will give him complete instructions. Plus, the neighbors always pitch in to help each other, if needed."

"I'm just a phone call away," Kelly reminded.

Calls, texts, emails, Zoom … the world had definitely gotten simpler to manage, in some ways, than when Sam was a young woman.

She set her phone down when she heard the oven timer. They dished up bowls of chile and settled at the table set for two, their little sanctuary amid the brewing storm.

"So, it looks like I can pack tonight, put the extra food in the freezer, and be ready to leave in the morning," she told him.

"Sounds perfect. I'll get Danny all squared away, right after dinner. The dogs can stay with him, out in the casita. Then I'll call Cecelia back."

Nellie, the border collie, perked her ears, somehow knowing Beau was talking about them. Being around Danny Flores meant extra treats. The guy was known to be a soft touch.

When Beau called his cousin back and told her they would be on the road, heading in her direction tomorrow, she sounded teary.

"Beau, I can't shake the feeling that there's more to it than a random act of violence, like the local cops are saying. Mark was onto something going on at work—the computer chip manufacturing plant here in Creston. I'm scared, Beau. There's always been talk of corruption … I don't know who to trust."

Samantha, slicing into a fresh-baked loaf of bread, looked over her shoulder, her keen eyes reading the tension in Beau's face. She placed the knife down gently and sealed the two halves of the loaf into plastic bags.

"Mark was digging into the company's dealings, and you think that got him killed?"

"Yes, I do," Cecelia's voice broke, a muffled sob

breaking her composure. "And I don't know what to do."

"Okay, Cece," Beau began, his tone firm yet comforting. "Keep quiet about your thoughts, locally. I want you to keep your head down until Sam and I get there. I'll look into it then."

"Thank you, Beau. Thank you!" The relief in Cecelia's voice was palpable. "Be safe, Beau. And … I'm sorry, for everything,"

He ended the call and turned toward Sam. "Guess we'd better get busy packing."

"Do you think it'll raise eyebrows, the sheriff returning home?"

"We're just visiting family, comforting my cousin in her time of need. As far as I know, not many in Creston today will know that I've been in law enforcement all these years. I was just a kid when we left."

"True." Sam finished tidying the kitchen while Beau called his ranch hand, Danny, and filled him in on the plan.

Upstairs, Sam pulled their travel bags from the closet, fondly remembering that their last big trip had been their honeymoon in Ireland. Such a lot had happened in their lives since then—her foray into the candy business, Kelly's marriage and the birth of their granddaughter, and the frightening drama surrounding the magic boxes. Her eyes were drawn to the dresser top, where the carved box held her jewelry. Better take that along to Oklahoma, she decided.

Beau came upstairs. "I took the dogs over to spend the night with Danny. No sense in getting them worried about us driving out in the morning. The minute I picked up their food bag they were completely on board and racing each other to the casita."

Sam chuckled, handing him one of the suitcases. He opened his dresser drawer and pulled out shirts, socks, and boxers.

"Hm." He handed Sam an old photograph. "It's Mark and Cecelia at some family barbecue. Must have been about the time they got engaged."

Mark's smile was wide, his arm slung easily around Cecelia's shoulders. She had big hair, very '80s, and his dark hair was collar-length. His brown eyes seemed intense, even in the casual setting.

Beau set the photo back in the drawer, closing it. "Mark was always knee-deep in some cause or another, fervent as a preacher sometimes. I wonder if he was still that way, not keeping quiet about things he didn't like at his workplace."

"That could explain a lot." Sam turned to the closet, pulling out one dressy outfit but keeping most of her choices casual. She couldn't imagine a town the size of Creston having too many places where she'd need to go fancy.

Within twenty minutes they'd filled both bags, and Sam had gathered a couple notebooks and her laptop, which she tucked into its case.

"I'll set these by the front door so we can get an early start," she said, "then I think I'm up for a hot chocolate. How about you?"

He nodded as she headed out of the bedroom. When they met up at the kitchen door a few minutes later, he beamed that winning smile at her. "I'm glad you're going with me."

"Looks like retirement's on hold, eh, cowboy?" Samantha's voice was steady, her support unwavering as she poured two mugs of steaming cocoa, the rich chocolate aroma wrapping around them like a comforting blanket.

They stepped out to the back deck, mugs in hand. Beau gazed out the window, where the vast New Mexico sky stretched endlessly above, a billion stars visible in the inky black. Tomorrow they'd trade the tranquility of Taos for the unknown of Creston, but for now, he'd savor the sweetness of home and hot cocoa.

Sam studied his face from the corner of her eye. Taking on a case, especially one outside his old jurisdiction, gave her a shiver of unease. But she could see the eagerness beneath his carefully guarded expression.

# Chapter 3

Not surprisingly, neither of them slept deeply and by five a.m. they were lying beside each other, wide awake. Without a word, they tossed the covers aside and began dressing. Sam had kept a box of muffins from the bakery, and they brewed coffee to fill a thermos. The quick breakfast would keep them going until they put some miles behind them.

"All right, Sheriff," Samantha chuckled. "Next stop, Creston."

He shot a quick glance in her direction at the use of his old title. "Next stop, Creston," he echoed, a dash of anticipation in his voice.

As they loaded their gear into the truck, the sun glowed behind Taos Mountain, glazing the New Mexico sky with hues of orange and red. The road stretched before them, an invitation for the case they were about to embark on. Sam settled into her seat, happy to have Beau do the driving this time.

"Enjoy the mountain scenery while you can," he said as they pulled onto the highway. "After the first hour, it gets pretty flat out there."

"We could stop in Angel Fire for a heartier breakfast," she reminded, knowing he was always up for eggs in some form. "I hear there are a couple of really good places there."

And there were. Forty minutes from home, they settled onto chairs at a cute bakery and soon had plates of huevos rancheros before them.

"Not to belittle your muffins, Sam, but this is more like what's it's gonna take to sustain me for the trip."

Sam just laughed. She was enjoying the break from her own cooking as well. The steaming plate of tortillas topped with beans, eggs, and green chile sauce hit the spot. Thirty minutes later they were back in the truck, making their way past Eagle Nest Lake, through the little town of the same name, then into the curving road of Cimarron Canyon. Beyond the town of Cimarron, the road did, indeed, straighten out and the scenery became nothing but open prairie.

"I think I'll see if I can dig up anything online that might be helpful," Sam said, pulling out her phone.

"Good. I'd be interested in seeing what the local news coverage said about Mark's death, if they published anything at all."

She tapped in some search words and came up with two mentions of Mark Mitchell in Creston, Oklahoma. One was a standard obituary, listing Cecelia Cardwell Mitchell as his surviving wife, no children. The other article was about the murder. Sam read through it quickly, then gave Beau the highlights.

"It's disappointingly short," she said. "Mark's name is barely mentioned. The story is mostly focused on a mugging in a parking garage. The local police chief is quoted as saying it was an unfortunate incident and there are few leads, but citizens of Creston can rest assured that the police are doing their utmost to solve this case."

"Basically, boosting his own ego and doing precious little."

"Right."

"Pretty much what Cece told me last night."

"I got the feeling she doesn't think very highly of the local cops." Sam closed her phone app and focused her eyes back on the road.

Beau gave a sigh. "Pretty much anybody who doesn't get the answers they want finds fault with law enforcement. I've been there a few times too, taking the blame for not solving a crime. So, I'm staying open on that question. We'll just have to see what we learn when we get there."

"But still, I'd go cautiously about what we say until we get a feel for the players, don't you think?"

He reached for her hand across the console. "Absolutely."

The miles peeled away and just past Clayton, they crossed the point where New Mexico, Texas, and Oklahoma meet. After that, Sam caught herself dozing until the next gas station stop in Guymon. The sun was well overhead now and she was pleased to see they were more than halfway there.

Beau stretched his shoulders as the gas pumped into the truck, and Sam offered to drive.

"I'm fine," he assured her. "Unless you really want to. The thing about the Oklahoma Panhandle, it's flat and the roads are straight. Not much of a challenge."

By the time she went inside and used the restroom, he was settled back in the driver's seat and she left it that way. Truthfully, it was nice not to be in charge, for once. She spent the next few minutes looking up the business where Mark had worked, Sterling Microchips. Their website touted what a wonderful company it was, with photos of smiling employees and the sterile room in the factory where you could probably eat scrambled eggs right off the floor (it didn't actually say that). The whole site was a PR dream. Other articles played up the generous support of charitable causes that Sterling Microchips was known for.

"If your cousin suspects someone at the company of being responsible for Mark's death, I'm thinking we want to be cautious about talking to folks at the newspaper," Sam said. "It seems they can't find enough wonderful things to say about the business."

"By the way you're smiling, I assume you're only half serious?"

"Maybe half. The other half of me is noticing how many ads Sterling seems to run in that paper."

"Everything with a grain of salt, right?" He turned his attention back to the road.

"So, tell me about Creston and what it was like growing up there."

Beau took a deep breath. "Well, in my day, the town was nothing more than a crossroads. Enid is the nearest city of any size, and it was an easy enough drive, so it's where nearly everyone went for their shopping and entertainment. The area, in general, is mainly known for wheat production and cattle. Enid is home to an Air Force base where a lot of pilots do their training. Creston had grain elevators and a spur of the railroad line so the wheat could be shipped out. Population was enough to support three elementary schools and one high school—go Sidewinders!"

"The Creston High Sidewinders? Kind of a mouthful." Sam laughed.

"Try that with an Oklahoma accent and you've got it."

"Hey, I grew up in West Texas. It took some real practice to lose the accent."

"Guess I escaped it at a young enough age," he said with a grin.

They passed roadside spots called Slapout and May, and Sam noticed cultivated fields that were still green, even in early November. "So, what would be the incentive for a big corporation to open a computer chip manufacturing plant out here?"

He shook his head. "I honestly don't know. Guess we'll find out more when we get there, which should be in …" He glanced at the dashboard clock. "… another half hour or so."

Beau's phone rang and Sam reached for it.

"Just wanted to let y'all know that I got called away and won't be home until a bit after five," came Cecelia's voice over the speaker. "And I forgot to leave a key out."

"No problem," Beau assured her. "We have a ways to drive yet and I'm sure we can entertain ourselves if we get there first."

She thanked him for being understanding about the mix-up and ended the call.

"Actually, I think we'll end up with at least an hour to kill," he told Sam. "I can give you the full town tour, but that's going to last all of ten minutes."

"It'll be fine. Maybe there's a park where we can stretch our legs."

Beau slowed the truck imperceptibly as they passed the sign that said Creston was three miles away. Grain elevators sat on the left side of the road, majestic in groups of three and four tall white cylinders. Until they came alongside them, the three-foot-high weeds around the bottom of each didn't show up well. But the road leading to the buildings was overgrown and the gate appeared permanently closed.

A chill skittered down Samantha's spine as they drove past the sad remains of what used to be the town's lifeblood. She could almost hear the echo of machinery and the bustle of workers now replaced by an oppressive silence.

"It's really gone downhill," Beau muttered, his gaze tracing the jagged lines of graffiti that marred the once proud structures. They passed a group of warehouses on the right, similarly abandoned and decrepit. "I bet these walls could talk."

"Let's hope they don't," Samantha replied, staring toward the rusted metal buildings. The stories held within those crumbling edifices were likely as dark as their soot-streaked exteriors.

Beau sped up and they came to a fresh sign with brightly painted colors: Welcome to Creston!

"That's better," Sam commented. "Maybe it's just that the economy has shifted from one sector to another."

"Whoa. I'd *say*." Beau was staring to the north, where a four-story behemoth of pristine concrete and blue-toned glass practically shouted its newness. He braked and whipped a quick left turn onto the lane leading to the building.

"I think we're seeing how the local economy has survived," Sam murmured.

The sign at the security entrance named it: Sterling Enterprises.

# Chapter 4

Back on the main drag, they passed a few more commercial businesses—a lumber yard, a self-storage complex, a bowling alley, and a fitness club—each clearly thriving better than those rusted warehouses on the outskirts.

"All this is new since I left," Beau commented, swiveling his head from left to right, taking it all in. "If we turn left up here, we'll pass my old school."

Sure enough, two blocks off the highway and a block east, sat an elementary school bounded by chain link fencing on three sides. The paint looked fresh, and the parking lot was full of cars.

"We attended K through 8 here," he said. "And the high school is just a little ..." Before he got the whole sentence out, they were approaching a larger building on the lefthand side. "Yep. Still here."

Sam smiled at the scary-looking image of a sidewinder snake on the side of the building that must be the gym. Go Sidewinders.

Beau cruised the length of the street, turned right, crossed the highway, and circled back to a classic small town square with a park at its center. A two-story, stone town hall held prominence at one end, and various small businesses ringed the other sides. Sam couldn't help but notice that nearly half of them had windows painted over or boarded up. She suppressed a shiver.

"It's probably been this way for twenty years," Beau said. "People will drive the fifteen miles into Enid to get to the big box stores and save a little money. Hard for local small businesses to survive."

"I suppose it's like that everywhere." She glanced at the clock. "Since we have an hour to kill before Cecelia gets home, what do you say we support the local coffee shop? I could do with a cup."

Beau's face lit up. "Gracie's Café … It's still here."

He eased his truck into a parking spot down the block and they opened their doors. A crisp breeze dissipated the stuffy air in the cab. Sam gazed out at Creston's nearly deserted sidewalks. "Was it always so … ghosty?" she muttered.

"It's definitely seen better days," Beau replied with a wry grin, stepping onto the curb, jamming his hands into his pockets as he took in the brick buildings, peeling trim paint, and weathered signs. His eyes scanned the area, alert to the hum of secrets hidden beneath the town's quiet façade. For all of Creston's outward peace and quiet, they had to keep in mind the reason they were here—a murder.

They locked the truck and set off side by side. Sam wrapped her cardigan tighter around herself, not just for the chill in the air but for the invisible weight of silence that seemed to press down from every closed shop window they passed. Whispers of the past seemed to cling to the bricks and mortar like ivy.

"Here we are. First stop, the local grapevine," Beau said, pausing outside Gracie's Café. "Let's keep our ears open and see if there's local gossip that may give us a clue or two as to what's going on around here."

Pushing through the café door, a bell chimed their entrance, cutting through the low hum of a half-dozen conversations. The smell of roasted beans mixed with the sweet tang of baked goods, a welcome reprieve from the hours on the road.

"Much better," Samantha sighed, as they approached the counter. The warmth of the café softened the edge of unease she'd picked up since arriving in Creston.

"Two coffees, please," Beau told the barista, a young woman with a cheery demeanor that seemed out of sync with the town's somber atmosphere. "Say, does Gracie still run this place?"

The young worker laughed. "She'd like to think so. But no. Grandma's pretty much homebound these days. Mama brings her in every couple days, to sit at her favorite table in the corner and let people fuss over her."

Beau chuckled. "I tend to forget I've been away almost forty years now."

"You have? Well, that's somethin'…" A bell dinged and the girl turned toward the call from the kitchen of "order up!" She told Beau she'd have their coffees out to them in a minute.

"Find us a spot?" he suggested to Sam, nodding toward the scattering of tables.

"Sure thing." She scanned the room, noting the mismatched chairs and local art adorning the walls. There was a charm here that felt authentic, a stubborn spark of life amidst the area's decay. She chose a table near the back, close enough to catch the undercurrent of local gossip that might help them thread together the story of Cecelia's husband—and whatever else lay hidden beneath Creston's quiet façade.

They settled at a table with a creaky leg, the worn wood whispering tales of countless previous occupants, and the girl showed up with two steaming mugs.

"Forgot to ask if you take cream," she said, setting them down. "My name's Janine. Holler if you need anything else."

"Well," Sam began. "I saw the sign about pie … What kinds do you have?"

Janine stared toward the ceiling, reciting from memory. "Today it's coconut cream, banana cream, chocolate, or blueberry."

"Ooh, coconut cream," Sam said.

"Two?" Janine gave a curious glance toward Beau.

"Two forks, one slice," he answered with a grin.

"And what if I didn't intend to share?" Sam teased after Janine walked away.

He gave her a look with his ocean blue eyes, the look that could get her to agree to anything. She blew him a kiss.

Voices from a nearby table caught their attention. Sam leaned back, her sleuthing instincts tuned to the conversations around them. Two old men in trucker caps were hunched over a checkerboard, their whispers slicing through the air.

"Another one gone," grumbled the first, his finger idly pushing a red checker across the board. "Like smoke, Earl. Just like smoke."

"Yup," Earl replied, his voice barely above a murmur. "And the Millers' boy saw somethin' strange near the creek last week. Lights or somethin'."

"Aliens?" The first man chuckled, but the laughter didn't reach his eyes.

"Harold, don't be a fool. It's this town—somethin' ain't right."

Samantha's eyes met Beau's. His brow was furrowed, but Janine stepped up just then with their pie and a carafe to top up their mugs. The old men's conversation was lost amidst the clink of coffee mugs and the subdued chatter around them.

"Did you hear that?" she whispered, nodding subtly toward the old timers, after Janine walked away.

"Enough to know we're not chasing shadows," Beau replied, taking a cautious sip from his mug.

The men's conversation turned back to their game, with one of them crowing about making a triple jump and claiming victory. They began packing up their checker board and settling their bill, shuffling toward the door. Two other tables had emptied since they arrived.

Sam's attention turned to the pie, which she could tell was made with freshly grated coconut and real cream. The crust was homemade, rich and buttery. She felt her eyes roll as the flavors hit her palate.

"Good pie," Beau mumbled through a mouthful. "You should get their recipe."

"Maybe I will."

"Excuse me, folks," came a gentle voice. They looked up to see a middle-aged woman, apron-clad, her smile warm but lined with the fatigue of hard years. "Name's Ellen, Janine's mama. Anything else I can get you folks?"

"Nice to meet you," Beau said, his charm surfacing effortlessly. "We're in town visiting family. Cecelia Mitchell is my cousin."

"Oh my. Yes, that poor little thing. Such a shock, what happened to her husband. I don't think they ever caught the person who did it."

Beau nodded somberly. "Cece's pretty shaken up by it. And then we just heard something about there being some disappearances. I'm wondering if there's some connection?"

Ellen paused, her smile fading slightly as she tucked a stray lock of hair behind her ear. "I wouldn't know, but it's a small town; when someone goes missing, we all feel it." Her gaze darted away for a brief moment, then back. "You know … Lucy Evergreen might be able to tell you more. She's got her ear to the ground, that one. Teaches the kids, knows their families, hears things."

"Lucy Evergreen?" Samantha echoed, feigning casual interest. "Would she be willing to talk to us, you think?"

"Can't say for sure, but she's a good soul. If there's help needed, Lucy's your gal." Ellen's affirmation was punctuated by the sound of the door chime as another patron left. A fleeting chill wafted in.

"Thank you, Ellen. We might just look her up," Beau said, offering a grateful nod.

"Anytime, hon." Ellen moved away, already summoning her customer-service smile for the next table.

"Looks like we've got our first lead," Beau murmured,

locking eyes with his wife.

"We'll have to find Ms. Evergreen," Sam agreed, the pieces of the puzzle urging her onward. "But right now we'd better be heading toward Cecelia's place. She'll be home by now."

They paid their tab and left a generous tip, then stepped out of the café, the bell chiming softly behind them. The crisp November air greeted them as they walked back to the truck. They exchanged a glance, both wondering about the veil of secrecy that seemed to shroud this little town.

Behind the wheel again, Beau reached into his pocket for the slip of paper where he'd written his cousin's address. "I don't remember this street name at all," he said, "but that's why we have a GPS onboard." He tapped a few buttons and a map came up.

The cheery voice led them away from the town square, across a bridge over the creek, and into a development with a decidedly new feel to it—Waverly Estates, according to the sign etched into stone at the entrance. These were not tract homes; each was large and elegant.

"Okay, this was definitely not here in my day," he said, his eyes growing wider.

They followed a tree-lined, divided road from which smaller residential streets branched out. At the fourth one, they were directed to turn left, and their destination would be straight ahead. It was a cul-de-sac and what stood straight ahead was—no other word for it—a mansion.

# Chapter 5

Holy moly. Mark must have been making some mega money in that job," Sam exclaimed when she saw the modern edifice with tall concrete pillars framing a wide porch and two-story entry. Mature trees and flowering shrubs gave it the impression of having been there a long time. In the looming dusk, subtle lighting highlighted the home's elegant features.

"Big house for a small town," Beau said, slowing as they approached Cecelia's home. It loomed before them, its grandeur surpassing the rest of the upscale homes in the development.

"Definitely not how I pictured her childhood home," Samantha replied, taking in the two-story elegance with a keen eye.

"Darlin' it's *nothing* like her childhood home, or any of

ours. I'm wondering if I have anything at all in common with my cousin, these days." He pulled into the driveway and cut the engine.

"Well, it looks like she's glad to see you," Sam said, moments before the woman who'd emerged from the front door raced up to the truck.

"Oh, Beau, I'm so happy you're here!" Cecelia grabbed him in a hug almost before his feet touched the ground. She seemed tiny beside Beau, a petite five-two, with her dark hair in a cute pixie cut. She wore fitted jeans and a V-neck tee in a shade of magenta that practically glowed.

Sam looked down at her own travel-wrinkled slacks and blouse. But Cece didn't seem to notice. She gave Sam the same huge hug she'd bestowed on Beau.

"Now, grab your stuff. I'll have supper on the table pretty soon."

"We weren't sure … I mean, we'd planned on getting a room somewhere," Sam said.

"Oh, don't be silly. Do you *see* this place? I'm bouncing around in there all by myself. I could house half the army—it's crazy." She turned to Beau. "I'd really like the company."

He placed an arm around her shoulders and gave a squeeze. "Of course. We'd love to stay."

Sam had to admit that being here would be way more luxurious than the Holiday Inn she'd spotted along the highway, and it would provide more opportunity for them to get the full story about Mark's death. As a lifelong insider here in Creston, Cecelia Cardwell Mitchell would probably know everyone and everything. She reached for her computer bag as Beau pulled out the suitcases.

"Ground floor or upstairs?" Cecelia asked as they

stepped into a foyer the size of their living room back home.

Sam shrugged. "Either is fine."

"Well, then I'm taking you to the best guest suite upstairs."

*There's a best suite?* Sam pasted her smile a little more firmly in place.

Cecelia took the smaller of the two bags from Beau and led the way up a floating staircase. A mezzanine opened up at the second level, with doors on two sides. They followed their hostess to a partially open doorway on the right.

"Here we go. We affectionately call this the green room."

A light switch to the left of the door revealed why. The cream-colored bedroom furniture was tastefully accented with bedding, wallpaper, and drapes in shades ranging from pale sage to deep forest. Clearly a professional designer had been involved.

Cece set down the small bag and turned on lamps, giving the room a warm, cheery glow, before she pointed out the en suite bath. It seemed to be stocked with high-end products, better than any posh spa Sam could imagine.

"Our room—" Cece's voice cracked a little and she took a deep breath. "My room—I'm in the west wing," she said with a little smile and a wave across the mezzanine. "But right now I'll go put the finishing touches on our dinner. It's nothing fancy, I warn you."

*Nothing fancy* turned out to be a heaping platter of fried chicken, bowls of potato salad, green salad, corn on the cob, and there was blueberry cobbler for dessert. Considering she'd done nothing but sit in the truck all day and had just shared a slice of pie an hour ago, Sam found herself surprisingly hungry once she smelled the food.

"I made the green salad myself," Cece admitted, "and the rest came from my favorite deli in Enid. They do chicken so much better than I ever could."

No explanation needed, Sam thought as they all dug in. No one talked much for a good fifteen minutes. When the cobbler came out, Beau shuffled in his seat and brought up the tough subject.

"Tell us what we can do for you, Cece," he began.

She stood at the granite counter and pulled three mugs from a cupboard. "Coffee, tea?"

Sam opted for chamomile and Beau accepted a decaf coffee from the K-cup selection.

Eventually, Cecelia settled at the table with a sigh. "I don't know that there's much you can do, Beau. I just felt I'd reached the end of my rope with the local authorities."

"Can you tell me what happened, from the beginning?"

"The night Mark died or further back than that?"

"We read the one article that indicated he was attacked in the parking garage at his place of work. That's about all we know, so include whatever you think is relevant. Everything."

"Understand, Mark was under a bunch of non-disclosure rules about the work they're doing out at Sterling. He was pretty good about keeping his work life separate from our personal life. We'd been busy, contracting this house for a couple years, then some travel. They were generous with time off, so we spent a few weeks in Europe, rode the train across Canada and up into the Rockies. But you don't want to know about that. So, let's see …" She drummed her fingers on the table for a moment.

"What was Mark's position in the company?" Sam asked.

"Accounting. Sterling Microchips is a division of

Sterling Enterprises, all housed within the same complex you probably spotted out there on the highway. Mark's work was mainly in the Microchips division. There are a couple dozen people in the department, and I'd say he was somewhere mid-level. More than a data entry guy, but nowhere near CFO."

Sam nodded.

"Something had been troubling Mark for several months. He never said specifically what, but it had to do with work. He would come home grouchy and get himself a stiff drink right away. Normally, we always spent a little time unwinding and we'd get into conversation about whatever was going on with the house or with one of my volunteer groups."

"Do you work outside the home?" Sam asked.

Cecelia shook her head. "One of the luxuries we gave ourselves was that I didn't have to commit to any nine-to-five job. Mark's salary supported us well, and his bonuses—well, that's what bought us this house. Sterling pays its people *very* generously. So, I volunteer at a women's shelter in Enid twice a week and serve on a couple of boards—the library and the arts council. That way, whenever we wanted to travel, I was free to just leave without limits on the time I could take."

"Sounds nice."

"It was." Her face became wistful. "I suppose I need to think about selling this house now. It's way too much for one person and I really can't afford the upkeep on the little portion of Mark's retirement I'll be receiving."

Beau shifted in his seat. "So, about the day Mark was killed … can you talk about that?"

Cecelia took a deep breath and cupped her coffee mug

with both hands. "The knock on the door came around eleven that night. He'd worked late. The building security guard had discovered Mark in the parking garage and called the police. It was Benny Padilla and Joe Sparling, guys I've known since high school, and I knew by their expressions it was something bad. They just said Mark had been attacked and stabbed to death in the garage there at work. When I asked questions, in the following days, I got the same story. Chief Benson felt it was a random mugging and Mark was in the wrong place at the wrong time. After repeating that to me a half dozen times, he began to imply that my husband shouldn't have been working so late. If he'd left the building at quitting time when everyone else did, he'd have been home at a decent hour."

"Blaming the victim," Sam whispered.

"Exactly."

"What about leads?" Beau asked. "Did they share anything from forensic reports, evidence at the scene … any of that?"

"Not a thing. And good luck getting Rollie Benson to talk. He kinda pats me on the hand and says there-there little lady, that type of stuff. I've thought about hiring this private investigator from Enid, Aiden Wilder. At this point it's just a name, someone I hope might not be involved with the locals, but I haven't taken the time or come up with the initiative to give him a call and set up an appointment."

"We stopped at the café on the square on our way in," Sam told her, "and some men in there were talking about the disappearance of somebody, like it wasn't the first person in town who has vanished. Have you heard anything about that? Any thoughts on whether those could be connected?"

Cece let out a shaky chuckle. "Lord, that's a whole other thing. I've heard the rumors, but none of the people who supposedly 'vanished' were in my own circle. You'd think, in a town of a thousand people, I'd know absolutely everybody, but I don't. So many are new, now that Sterling opened the plant. And lots of their employees come from the surrounding towns around here, even Enid, so I see a lot of unfamiliar faces these days." She paused and stared into her mug. "I never really connected those disappearances with what happened to Mark. Do you really think there's something to it?"

Beau shrugged. "No idea. But I learned not to write off seemingly unrelated events until I can check them out."

Sam met Cece's gaze. "At the café, someone mentioned the name of a local teacher, Lucy Evergreen. Said we should talk to her."

"That might be a smart idea. One of the men who vanished left a family here, and I'm pretty sure I heard one of the kids was in high school. Lucy would know."

Beau yawned, apologizing, but Sam realized how tired they both were.

"Y'all need to get to bed," Cecelia told them, standing and gathering the empty mugs. "We'll have plenty of time to go over questions tomorrow, when we're all a lot fresher."

They said goodnight and made their way back to their luxurious bedroom. "I'll wait until morning to actually unpack," Sam said, grabbing her toothbrush and setting the carved box on top of the dresser.

Beau stepped into the shower while she brushed her teeth. Ten minutes later, they crawled between the soft sheets. "Not much to go on yet, with our new case," he said as he pulled the blanket up to his shoulders.

Our new case. Sam smiled, turning to switch off the lamp. She'd heard the excitement in his voice.

# Chapter 6

The morning sun cast a soft glow across the schoolyard as Samantha and Beau arrived.

"She's in class right now," the receptionist told them after looking at Beau's identification, "but her free period is next hour. If you want to wait around for twenty minutes, you can."

They got Lucy's room number and decided to wander the grounds while they waited.

Shouts from the football field filled the air as they circled the gym, momentarily pushing away the gloom that seemed to hang over the town. Beau paused, watching the players gather and hang on their coach's words. Although they couldn't make out the specifics, it was evident the boys were getting a pep talk before the coach blew his whistle and dismissed them. Twenty kids thundered past, on their way to the showers.

"Lot of memories in that," Beau commented as they made their way back into the classroom building.

Outside Lucy's room, they peered through the window, spotting a slim woman with graying hair who was probably in her early sixties. She seemed to have the full attention of every student as she held up a novel and engaged them in some kind of discussion.

"Passionate about her subject," Beau said, nodding appreciatively.

They waited until the bell rang, watching as Lucy's students filed out, her voice following them with a reminder about their homework. Beau took the lead, stepping forward as Lucy began to gather her papers.

"Ms. Evergreen?" He extended a hand, which she shook. "I'm Beau Cardwell, and this is my wife, Samantha. We're friends of Cecelia Mitchell."

"Friends? Or related—there's not many Cardwells left in town but I do remember a few of them."

"Okay, related," he admitted with a laugh. "We're cousins."

"Ah, yes, I heard Cecelia recently lost her husband," Lucy responded, her voice steady despite the flicker of concern that crossed her features. "How can I help?"

Beau's demeanor softened. "We're here looking into some things. Unsolved disappearances, but especially what happened to Mark Mitchell." He watched Lucy closely, noting the way her eyes narrowed just slightly, an intelligent spark behind them.

"Of course," Lucy said, her curiosity piqued. "I'll help if I can, but I really have no idea what was behind Mark's death. Only what I heard in the news." Her gaze shifted from Beau to Samantha.

Lucy tamped down the stack of papers, her eyes never leaving their faces. "Those disappearances though," she murmured, almost to herself, "and sudden fortunes sprouting overnight." She set the papers aside, a furrow etching her brow. "It's set everyone on edge."

"Fortunes? You mean the new subdivisions, the big houses?" Samantha leaned in closer, her curiosity piqued.

"That's some of it. And I understand about the huge salaries they're paying out at Sterling. That company really did bring a boom to our little economy here," Lucy clarified, tucking a strand of hair behind her ear. "But those elevators and warehouses," she gave a nod toward the window where the skeletal structures loomed in the distance, "those were the heartbeat of Creston once. Jobs for everyone. Then the recession hit, and it was like watching dominoes fall."

She sighed, her slender frame sagging ever so slightly with the burden of memory.

"Left us in a bad spot, huh?" Beau said, his voice low.

"More than a bad spot," Lucy replied. "It birthed corruption in the shadows. Some people, desperate to survive, made choices—dark choices. We used to pull together here, to have a real sense of community. Now, some folks are flashing cash like they've struck oil, but there's no oil here anymore. Just a whole lot of secrets ..." Her voice trailed off with the weight of her words.

"Secrets, such as?" Beau's question hung heavy in the air.

"More than usual for a town this size. Accidents, they say, *disappearances*, but ..." Lucy hesitated, her gaze darting to the closed door as if half-expecting someone to barge in.

"Go on," Samantha urged gently.

Lucy sighed. "Two of my students. Since the start of the school year, there've been two families whose circumstances changed overnight. The mother or dad's gone, the kids are pulled from school the next day without explanation or goodbye. We never used to see things like that. I can't really say what actually happened. I hear the rumors but I can't say as I *know* much of anything. Be careful, though. Some stones in Creston are better left unturned."

Beau nodded. "We'll tread lightly. Thanks, Lucy." He smiled, but the smile didn't quite reach his eyes.

"Lucy, we can't thank you enough," Samantha said, her words genuine and warm. "Your insight's been invaluable."

"If you hear anything more, even through the grapevine, would you let us know?" Beau watched the teacher closely, trying to gauge her reaction.

Lucy paused, the sunlight from the window casting a lattice of light and shadow across her desk. Her eyes held a flicker of uncertainty as she looked from Beau to Samantha and back again. She bit her lip and took a deep breath.

"Okay, of course I'll help," Lucy finally conceded. "But we need to be careful. I can't do or say anything that would put my students in danger."

"Absolutely." Samantha took her hand, feeling a thread of camaraderie.

"Thank you, Lucy. Really," Beau added, offering her a grateful smile as they turned to go.

The air outside was crisp, and they walked with a brisk pace, back to the parking lot where Beau's truck waited.

"What do you think?" Sam asked as he started the engine.

"I think she has a motive to be helpful. I sense she

genuinely cares for her students and the people here in town. Knowing of two families who left suddenly, she'll want us to get to the bottom of it before it happens again."

"You think it will happen again?"

"We heard those two old guys yesterday in the café. They said right out—another one vanished. That tells me it's an ongoing thing."

Sam nodded. "So, where to next?"

"I'm debating between a visit to the local cops, find out what Rollie Benson has to say. Either that or reach out to this private investigator Cece mentioned."

"May I suggest we give a call to Aiden Wilder, the PI, first. Set up an appointment." She was already tapping a search on her phone. "Then we drop in at the Creston PD and see if we get anything at all from the chief. My guess is that we'll get the same story he's been giving your cousin."

"I'll go in with my retired-sheriff credentials first, before I even admit I'm related to Cece and Mark. Maybe that'll net us something. And I completely agree with the idea of talking to Wilder. Could be he's already working on some aspect of this, maybe for another client."

Beau steered out of the high school parking lot, heading toward the town square, while Sam hit the link for Aiden Wilder's phone. He answered on the second ring and she put the phone on speaker as she introduced herself and Beau. She gave the quick gist of the reason for the call, saying they were in town to help Beau's cousin find some answers.

"Are you available for a meeting, say, in an hour?" Wilder's voice sounded young and professional. At her affirmative, he continued. "There's a little restaurant on the outskirts of Enid, no more than fifteen minutes from the east end of Creston. Rosie's. Can we meet there at eleven?"

"Perfect."

Beau edged the truck into a diagonal parking space in front of the town hall as Sam ended the call.

"Okay, let's see what kind of reception we get from the local constabulary," he said, reaching into the back seat for his Stetson.

He set the hat on his head as they walked toward the main entrance of the two-story building. Inside, signs directed visitors toward Administrative Offices on the right, Motor Vehicles on the left, and Police Department straight ahead, down a long hallway. Before a set of double doors, a uniformed officer sat at a desk. Beau flashed his official ID, with the word Retired imprinted at the top, and asked to speak with Chief Benson.

The desk officer apparently didn't have the authority to turn him down. He picked up the phone. "Chief, there's a retired lawman here from New Mexico to see you."

The answer apparently was affirmative, as the officer rose and pushed one side of the double doors open. "Second door on the left."

Rollie Benson sat behind a large desk and took his time closing a manila folder and slipping it into a drawer before looking up to meet Beau's eyes.

"Come on in," he said, standing. His dark uniform shirt strained a bit across the large gut, and there was an obvious grease stain on his tie. His fingers were tobacco stained, and a coffee mug with an oily skim on the surface gave the small room a stale reek.

Sam held back, noting the details, as Beau shook the man's hand. Benson gestured for them to take the two chairs in front of his desk.

"What brings you to Creston, Chief?"

"Sheriff. Retired from Taos County."

Benson nodded slowly. "Never been there myself." He glanced at his cold coffee, then back at the visitors. "You folks here on vacation?"

"Visiting kinfolks," Beau said. "Turns out there's a connection with a murder here in town and I said I'd ask around."

"Well, as you can imagine, we don't get too many murders in a town this size." Rollie Benson's smile revealed yellowed teeth and gave Sam a queasy feeling.

Beau nodded. "Yeah, we're from a small town too. But stuff happens everywhere these days. This wasn't your usual drunk-in-a-bar or drug-deal-gone-sideways, though. Mark Mitchell. Pretty upstanding citizen, from what I hear."

"And how did you hear this?"

Beau ignored the question. "It sounds like the case got closed pretty quickly. So the forensics reports must be available. I'd like to take a look at those."

Benson lost his friendly, good old boy demeanor right away. "Sorry. Can't do that."

"Professional courtesy usually extends to other jurisdictions, to other law enforcement that might have an interest in seeing a case solved."

"We solved it."

"No one was arrested. It seems no suspects were seriously considered for it."

Benson put the smile back on his face. "Look, you know as well as I do that some cases just never do result in an arrest. There's not enough evidence, no viable suspects … they go cold."

"But they remain unsolved. I'd like the chance to go through the file, just see if I can pick up on anything."

"Well, sure. Sure." The chief stood, a clear signal. "Put in a request, go through channels, fill out the paperwork. I'm sure we can accommodate you."

Beau sent a pointed glance toward the file cabinet in the corner, but the other man didn't relent. Not even a little. Sam felt herself seething inside.

"If that's all, Sheriff, I've got another appointment in five minutes."

Sam didn't think she imagined the smirk on the face of the desk officer as they walked out. Had the little weasel kept the intercom line open and listened in?

"A cold case? In less than two months?" she demanded, once she and Beau were back in his truck. "That man was completely odious."

Beau chuckled. "Odious. That's good. And it's apt. But it was pretty clear he was going to stonewall."

"Which tells us something, right? There's probably evidence in that file, something important."

"Maybe, maybe not. My guess is that he's worried an experienced lawman would spot shoddy police work, might report him to somebody higher up."

"So, what do we do now?"

"Let's meet with that private investigator and see where that takes us."

# Chapter 7

Rosie's Restaurant sat on the highway as they neared Enid, exactly where Aiden Wilder had told them to find it. The bright turquoise paint was fresh, the landscaping well tended, and the parking lot was full—all the signs of a popular and successful eatery. A chalkboard sign in front said today's special was pot roast with potatoes, gravy and green beans. They walked in and were greeted by a wave of heavenly, meaty aroma—a good recommendation for the pot roast.

A young man, sitting alone at a four-top table, spotted them and waved. He was in his late twenties, seeming mature for one so young, with short black hair impeccably cut, his athletic build obvious even beneath the casual attire of jeans and a button-up shirt.

"Mr. Cardwell, is it?" he said, extending his hand.

"Beau's fine," he said, taking the offered handshake. Aiden's grip was firm, confident—a silent testament to his character. Beau turned to introduce Sam.

"Yes, Sam. We spoke. I believe you said you're looking into Mark Mitchell's unfortunate end." Aiden's smile was warm.

She nodded. "When we talked, you didn't seem surprised."

"Yeah, okay, I have to admit that I'd already heard it around town."

"Word travels fast," Beau remarked.

"Like wildfire," Aiden agreed as they took seats around the table.

"Probably explains why I got nowhere with the police chief just now." The townsfolk were proving to be as interconnected as the roots of the ancient oaks lining Main Street. "Did Sam mention that we're also curious about the various people who've disappeared in recent months? Somehow it feels to me like those might be connected."

A waitress in a black t-shirt with the restaurant logo appeared like magic. Beau opted for the pot roast special, while Sam went along with Aiden's choice of a barbeque pork sandwich. Once their iced teas were delivered, Aiden settled back in his chair. "Now, what can I do to help?"

His gaze was steady, the earnestness in his eyes reflecting a fire that Beau recognized in himself—a real need to put things right.

"Helping out of the goodness of your heart?" Beau asked, his tone light but probing.

"Well, I do have an hourly rate, which we will discuss. But mainly, Mark's story left a bad taste in my mouth. I don't like loose ends. I think that comes from my experience as an MP in the Air Force, stationed at the base here. My tour was up, I got my PI license, and it's been my life ever since. I know you're thinking this guy's pretty young, and that's true. But I've worked some fairly complex cases. The military was excellent training for dealing with bureaucracies, on both sides of the coin."

"I don't like loose ends either, and this one really bothers me because it's a family member," Beau admitted. Sam, who had been quietly observing, saw the corner of her husband's mouth twitch—an almost-smile that signaled his interest was piqued. Aiden just laughed softly, the sound rich and confident.

"Then it looks like we've got ourselves a common goal, Beau."

Their food arrived just then, and they dug in while sharing bits of history. Aiden's upbringing in West Texas didn't surprise Sam; she'd caught that distinctive drawl from the beginning. Another thing the two had in common was leaving home at a young age because of friction with parents and with the lifestyle at home. Beau described his years in Taos as sheriff as being the most satisfying work he'd ever done. Again, Sam caught the hint that he'd missed law enforcement more than he'd let on.

"You know, together I think we can unravel this mystery," Aiden said, pushing his empty plate back, the vibrant energy in his voice matching the spark in his eyes.

"Agreed," Beau said, nodding. "Two heads are better than one, especially in a town where secrets are as well-kept as family recipes."

"Sounds like you've got experience with small-town skeletons," Aiden observed, a knowing look crossing his features.

"More than I'd care to admit," Beau responded with

a wry grin. Samantha felt a ripple of excitement at the teamwork unfolding before her. She knew Beau had a knack for sifting through lies to find the bedrock of truth, and with Aiden's help, they could tackle the tough questions around here.

Beau leaned back in his chair, studying Aiden Wilder with a mix of curiosity and respect. The man had an air about him that spoke of unsolved puzzles and late-night stakeouts, the kind that only come with years of experience in the field.

"I think I'd rather discuss the specifics of the case in a more private setting," he said, eyeing the crowded room. The noise level was probably such that no one would overhear, but knowing how quickly gossip spread around here, he'd rather not take the chance.

"My office? It's about six blocks away," Aiden said, reaching for the check, which the waitress had left behind.

They followed his lead, and in less than ten minutes were sitting in an immaculate office in a small strip mall nearby. "I keep things low-key," he'd said as he unlocked the door. "Basically, I'm a one-man operation. Why go fancy? I answer my own phone, type my own emails, and unless things get really complicated, I can usually handle the background and research without much other assistance."

"So," Beau started, tapping a finger on the neat desktop, "how do you think we should start?"

"As far as the disappearances go, I'm already putting out feelers," Aiden replied, casually rolling a pen between his fingers. "I've built up a network that's pretty solid— contacts in law enforcement at the state and national level, tech geniuses, you name it."

Beau nodded, impressed despite himself. "That could

come in handy around here."

"Absolutely," Aiden agreed, his eyes brightening. "You'd be surprised what people are willing to share when they know you can keep a secret."

Samantha watched the exchange, a smile tugging at her lips. She knew Beau valued loyalty and skill above all else, and it seemed like Aiden was offering both in spades. The two men veered off into a sort of who's who in the area, with Beau remembering a surprising number of names, considering he was a young teen when his family left. Aiden, for his part, showed respect for their twenty-year difference in ages. She got the feeling he was learning from Beau, as well.

Beau leaned back in his chair. "I like your resources," he began, the hint of a drawl coloring his words, "my gut's usually my best tool. But your expertise? That's the edge we've been lacking, coming here almost as strangers."

"Two heads are better than one, right?" Aiden quipped, his lips quirking up at the corners. "Especially when they're not thinking the same old thoughts."

"Exactly." Beau tapped the side of his head. "You've got the tech and contacts. I've got the long-term experience. Together, we cover all bases."

Samantha nodded from her seat beside her husband, her eyes flicking between the two men. "And different angles mean fewer blind spots," she added.

"So, Aiden, can you send me a list of the most recent disappearances, everything from, say, six months before Mark's death? I'm thinking you should keep working the angle of the disappearances, and Sam and I can start asking more questions around Mark's activities. I'm especially interested in what was going on around his workplace."

"Agreed. I'll … what's best? Email?"

Sam nodded, letting him know she'd brought her laptop.

"Okay, I'll email you the basic who-what-where-when, along with my notes specific to each disappearance. Had you thought about where you would start? Whom you wanted to talk to?"

"Not much, beyond today. Cecelia doesn't know many details about Mark's job at Sterling Microchips. It was all pretty hush-hush. So, I'm thinking I need some background, some idea of where to start out there."

"You know who might be a big help there? Talk to Ethan Hawthorne at the Creston Library. It's a fairly small place, as libraries go. Privately funded, I think. But they've got lots of local resources. He could probably find out more for you about Sterling, things the company website doesn't necessarily go into."

"Good idea. Is that the little library on Sixth Street?" Beau asked, standing.

Aiden nodded. "Same location. I suspect they've fancied it up a bit in recent years, but yeah, that's the place."

"We're on it," Sam said as they headed toward the front door.

* * *

Back in Creston they located the library easily. Aiden was right—the place was small, but once they walked inside, Sam could see that it was well stocked. Immediately to the right of the front desk was a cozy children's section and beyond that were rows of shelved fiction. The lefthand side of the room held nonfiction and several computers for the use of their patrons.

Beau's eyes immediately swept across the quiet space. The scent of old books and a faint trace of lemon furniture polish filled the air. His gaze met Sam's, sharing their mutual love of libraries; they were like treasure troves for the inquisitive mind. Shelves lined with wisdom from floor to ceiling, people lost in worlds between pages … and today, they hoped one of those shelves held potential keys to their puzzle.

"Let's see," Beau muttered under his breath, adjusting the brim of his Stetson. Samantha pointed to their left.

There, peeping from between aisles of history and biographies, was a solitary figure that matched the description they had been given: messy brown hair that might be the result of careful styling (or not), glasses perched on the bridge of a nose buried in a book.

"Excuse me," Sam called out. "You wouldn't happen to be Ethan Hawthorne?"

The slight man regarded them carefully, a hint of surprise flickering behind the lenses. The visitors stepped forward and introduced themselves, letting the librarian know it was Aiden Wilder who suggested they stop by.

Ethan's smile seemed reserved. "Please, have a seat," he said, his voice soft but clear as he led them to a small seating area near the back of the room, in the periodicals section. "Aiden probably told you I'm Creston's walking encyclopedia or some such thing. He may give me too much credit."

"Thanks," Beau replied, the creases around his eyes deepening as he settled into the offered chair. The wood creaked a little, somehow adding to the library's charm.

He leaned forward, elbows resting on the arms of his

chair, and met Ethan's gaze. "I grew up here in Creston, but since my family left when I was a kid, I feel like there's a lot I don't know. It's not just the good ol' days, though." He paused, letting a silent beat pass between them. "Sometimes the past has a way of creeping into present troubles. Like the unfortunate business with the murder case we got on our hands."

"Murder case?" Ethan's expression remained composed, yet there was a flicker in his eyes, the kind that spoke of gears turning and pieces falling into place. Beau recognized that look; Samantha always had it right before she unraveled some mystery or another.

"We've been asked to look into the death of Mark Mitchell," Sam added. "His wife, Cecelia, thinks there's more to it than the simple conclusion the police came to. Maybe something connected with Mark's work."

"Oh, yes, Cecelia." Ethan's fingers stilled on the spine of the book he'd carried over, a slight arch forming in his brow. The book thudded softly as he set it on an end table, dust motes dancing in the slant of light from the nearby window. He leaned in, his chair giving a faint squeal of protest.

"You know my cousin, then?" Beau studied the other man's face.

"Since our school days. And now that you mention she's your cousin, I definitely see the resemblance." Ethan's smile widened. "I'm sorry I didn't remember you sooner."

"No reason to. As I mentioned, my parents and I moved away before I was in high school. Albuquerque, then up north to Taos."

"Ah. I see."

"Circling back to Mark's place of employment," Sam

mentioned, "maybe there are local news stories … rumors … something we didn't pick up from the recent news?"

"Creston wasn't always so …" Ethan gestured vaguely, encompassing the quiet that hung between the stacks. "… sleepy. We had a heartbeat once, businesses bustling, Main Street alive."

"I recall," Beau nodded, his eyes reflecting a sentimentality for a past he too remembered fondly.

Sam sat back, realizing this was a man who wanted to start every story at the beginning. And perhaps there would be some clues in his recollections.

"Indeed," Ethan said, pushing his glasses up the bridge of his nose. "The recession hit us hard. Mom-and-pops closed doors, their dreams shuttered tight. It was a cascade, one after the other." His hands sketched the rise and fall, like a graph chart of the local economy.

"Sad to see that happen to good folks," Beau replied, the words tinged with genuine regret.

"More than sad, it was a transformation," Ethan continued, a professorial glint appearing behind the lenses of his glasses. "It changed the fabric of our town, wove in threads of desperation where there used to be hope."

"Desperation can lead people to do strange things," Sam mused, wondering if those same threads might tie into the tangle of the current investigation.

She found herself focusing on his every word, every gesture, watching for potential clues waiting to be unearthed. He leaned back, fingers tapping a silent rhythm on the chair arm.

"Desperation," Beau echoed, his mind already piecing together fragments of Creston's downturn with the grim puzzle of the murder case. "Leads to corners cut, laws bent … sometimes broken."

"Exactly," Ethan agreed, pushing his glasses up again. They stubbornly slipped down his nose again. "Rumors have it that some people took shortcuts. Unsavory ones."

Sam met his gaze.

"I overhear a lot of things here in the library. People don't realize how whispers carry in the quiet." He gave a rueful grin. "And out in public, sometimes I feel like the invisible guy. When you're eating alone in a restaurant, people carry on with the most intimate conversations as if you're not even there."

"Shortcuts?" Beau reminded gently, not wanting Ethan to lose his train of thought.

"Whispers of embezzlement," Ethan said, voice low as if the books around them could hear. "Bribery too. It's like the recession opened a Pandora's box. People changed."

Sam's ears practically twitched. This was it, the juicy bit of Creston lore that might just provide their first solid leads. "And this … would it relate to Mark's place of work, by any chance?"

"Ah, the computer chip plant." Ethan's nod was slow, deliberate. His finger traced the spine of the book he'd set aside. "A beacon of modern industry amidst our troubles, yet not immune to scandal."

"Scandal? What type?" The word felt electric on Beau's tongue.

"Allegedly," Ethan added quickly, eyes darting around as though someone might overhear. "A few employees, they talked. About things not adding up. Numbers, shipments. You know how it is."

"Of course," Beau replied, his sheriff's instincts flaring to life. Mark's workplace was now more than a backdrop;

it was a stage where shadowy things seemed to have happened.

Beau leaned in, eyes narrowing with focus. "Could Mark have stumbled onto something … dangerous, while sniffing around?"

"Perhaps," Ethan murmured, the word laced with caution. "From what I gather, Mark had a knack for numbers—saw patterns where others saw chaos. He might've dug too deep, found threads no one was meant to pull."

"Threads leading to his death?" Beau's voice was soft, but the gravity of his words hung between them.

"Sadly, it's not a stretch." Ethan's toe tapped on the wooden floor, betraying a nervous energy. "The plant's always been a bit of an enigma. Deals behind closed doors, you know?"

"Mark liked puzzles, all right," Beau mused aloud, thinking back on things Cecelia had told him. He shifted gears, his law enforcement background kicking in. "What about the folks running the show? Any whispers about the executives?"

Ethan hesitated, then leaned closer. "I don't know specifics. But there's chatter. Disgruntled workers, hushed arguments overheard in break rooms. It's not just the machinery humming with secrets."

"Got it," Sam said, filing away every hint, ever vigilant.

Ethan's nod was slow, deliberate. "Jason Blackwood is one of them. A shark in a suit. There's talk that he doesn't play by the rules—backroom deals, coercion tactics. He's a cool one, though. The public side appears squeaky clean."

"Blackwood, huh?" Sam leaned back, her mind racing, forming an image she didn't much care for.

"Again, this is mostly rumor, things I've overheard. More than a few folks have rubbed elbows with him and come away worse for it," Ethan continued, pushing his glasses up once again. "If there's a shadow cast over this town, he's at the center, casting it."

"Appreciate you sharing, Ethan." Beau offered a grim smile.

Sam could see that his old instincts were flaring up, that cop sense tingling. "Any chance we can loop you in if we hit a wall? We really could use someone who's up to date with the pulse of this town."

"Of course," Ethan replied without missing a beat. His reserve gave way to a flicker of excitement at being included. "I've got books, records … a whole library at my disposal. Just say the word."

"Thanks so much." Beau sat straighter his seat, smiling, showing a kinship with the quiet librarian.

Ethan beamed, an earnest glint in his eye. "Whatever you need, Beau, Sam. Information is just part of it." His voice grew firmer, a hint of steel beneath the scholarly veneer. "I believe in right and wrong. If I can help put things to rights, then that's what I'll do."

"Good man," Beau said with a nod, feeling a surge of gratitude. He always respected a strong spine in folks.

"Justice matters," Ethan added, almost to himself. The words weren't just lip service; they were a promise from a man who spent his life surrounded by stories of heroes and villains, knowing which side he aimed to be on.

"Counting on it," Beau replied, a half-grin spreading across his face. He stood up, the chair scraping softly against the library's wooden floor.

Sam felt pleased because Beau was pleased. They'd

found some allies in this town full of stonewallers, and they'd got a solid lead on the types of irregularities Mark might have been uncovering at Sterling.

They slipped past the rows of bookshelves, as two women and three kids entered, greeting Ethan enthusiastically. The chatter of the library faded as they pushed through the front doors and down the library steps.

Sam could see it in her husband's demeanor. New leads were swirling in his head, each one a thread he was itching to pull, and a renewed determination was firing up within him. Beau Cardwell was back on the hunt.

# Chapter 8

The sun cast a long shadow beside Beau's truck when they got in and pulled out of the library's parking lot.

"You up for a trip out to Sterling Microchip, try to track down this Jason Blackwood guy?" Beau asked.

"Are you?"

"I think it's been a long day already and we've got a lot to process. I'll be fresher and sharper in the morning."

Sam appreciated the caring look he sent her way. She gave a gentle laugh. "I was hoping you'd say that. Plus, we haven't checked in with Cecelia all day. I think we should share what we've learned and see if she can add to it."

"That's my smart deputy," he teased.

They arrived at the huge house a few minutes later and used the key Cece had given them to let themselves in.

"Hello?" Sam called out. "We're back."

A soft sound and a mumble came from an archway on the left, a massive living room they'd barely noticed the night before. The room held three groupings of sofas and chairs, a grand piano, and a glassed-in fireplace that was now dark and cold. Behind the top of a white sofa, Sam caught a glimpse of Cecelia's dark hair. She tapped Beau's forearm and motioned in that direction.

"Cece? You okay?" he asked, holding back from entering the room.

"Yeah … *no* …" A loud sniff and the sound of a lengthy nose-blow into a tissue. "I'll be—" Cecelia stood with her back to them and spent a moment tugging at the bottom edge of her emerald green tunic top, smoothing her jeans. When she turned, her puffy eyes and reddened nose showed, even at a distance. "I'm sorry. I'm such a mess."

They both moved toward her, Sam reaching out to take her newest cousin into her arms. "Hey, that's understandable."

"Would you rather be alone?" Beau asked.

Cece shook her head. "I shouldn't be. I need a distraction." She glanced at her watch. "I'm declaring it happy hour. Let's go to the kitchen and rustle up something to eat, and you can tell me about your day."

She led the way into her immaculate kitchen and opened the refrigerator doors wide.

"We can take you out for dinner if you don't want to cook," Beau suggested.

"Oh heavens no. Look at all this food. I went a little crazy at the store when you said you were coming." She began pulling out cheeses, sliced deli meats, olives, and hummus. Within three minutes she had a decent sized charcuterie board going. "And then I've got steaks, pork chops, ribs … tons of choices for dinner later."

Sam's eyes widened. "Really, the snacks will be plenty. Beau downed a big pot roast meal at lunch time. And we're used to lighter fare at night. Tomorrow we'll go with a smaller lunch and probably be ready for one of those steaks." It was clear their hostess had gone to a lot of trouble to be ready to feed them substantially.

"Sounds good. Now, Beau, over there are the booze and mixers. And wine is that way," she said with a gesture vaguely toward a bank of cabinets.

Sam followed the suggestion, pulling on a sleek gold door-pull to discover a chilled compartment with a veritable wine closet behind it. "Say you didn't buy all of this on account of us."

"Sorry, no. Mark was the wine connoisseur in the house. He loved visiting wineries wherever we went and always brought home a case or two. When we entertained, it came in handy. I have no idea what I'll do with it now. I'm more of a bourbon and Coke kind of girl. Help yourself to all you want."

Sam studied the bottles, noticing Beau had picked up the hint and was pouring bourbon for himself and their hostess. Sam chose a pinot noir, thinking it would go well with the cheeses, and found an opener. When she uncorked it, she discovered Mark had a special aerator that fit into the bottle top. Life really was good when you had the money to do it this way.

Then she checked herself. Life was good when you were alive to savor it. And poor Mark had lost that chance. She swallowed hard, took a breath, and poured her wine before turning back to the others.

They took seats at the kitchen island and clinked glasses. Cece was looking livelier, more *present* than earlier.

"So, I really do wanna hear about y'all's day. Did you get anything out of Rollie Benson?"

"Only an instruction that we would need to fill out a request form to see any of the police or forensic reports," Beau said, his mouth twisting at the side.

"Oh, that big patoot. He's just such a … a …" Cecelia set her glass down with a hard clunk.

"You don't need to come up with a stronger word," Sam assured her, grinning. "We probably already said them all, as we were driving away."

"We had lunch with the private investigator from Enid, the one you mentioned. He's trying to learn more about the disappearances," Beau said. "And we talked with Lucy Evergreen at the school."

"My, you two have been busy!"

"And we spoke this afternoon with Ethan Hawthorne, the librarian."

"Ah, Ethan … Did I ever tell you he was sweet on me for about five minutes, back in high school?" Cece's expression softened. "Course, I dated a few guys but my heart always belonged to Mark. We never made it a *steady* thing until we got to college though."

She straightened in her seat and reached for another slice of the smoked gouda on the board. "Anyway. All that's *way* old news. Tell me something new."

They recapped the gist of each conversation, ending with their plan to drive out to Sterling Microchips in the morning to see if they could learn anything there.

"We thought we'd start with Jason Blackwood. Was his job directly connected with Mark's—do you know?"

Cece shook her head, thinking. "I doubt it. I only met Mr. Blackwood a coupla times, at company Christmas parties, I think. He's a looker. Unfortunately, he knows it. You know that vibe you get when a guy is just totally full of himself. I don't know. That's just my impression. Mark thought he was super smart—believed everything on the resume, I suppose. Other people seem to like him okay."

"Good to know." Beau noticed Cece's drink was low and offered to make her another.

"I'd like some more background," Sam said, rising. "I'll get my laptop."

When she came back from upstairs, she found that her husband had also topped up her wine glass. She opened the computer and had another cracker with garlic hummus while it booted up. Wiping her hands on a napkin, she typed Jason Blackwood into the search bar.

Aside from a real estate agent somewhere in Florida, all the results seemed to be about the man they knew about, and most of those links went to his role at the big chip manufacturing firm. There was one link to a profile on LinkedIn, but Sam discovered it was a rehash of his official credentials at the company.

"Looks like he keeps his private life fairly private," she commented, her eyes scanning the screen. "Professionally, he's second in command, after Olivia Sterling herself. Vice President of Operations. I see what you mean about his looks. His professional photo has a preening sort of vibe. Olivia is a beautiful woman too. Maybe that's part of the job criteria out there. Although that can't be the whole story. Blackwood has degrees from Harvard, Stanford, and Wharton. That's definitely top-of-the-top."

"Way out of my league, with my bachelor's from a state

university," Cecelia commented.

Sam's attention went to her email tab, where a slew of messages had come in while she was out all day. She clicked over to it. Amid the ads and junk she spotted one from Kelly (miss you already, hope you're having fun!), one from Becky at the bakery (all's fine here, do not worry!), and one from Aiden Wilder.

Hmm. She opened his note and saw there was an attachment, a spreadsheet.

"Efficient," she murmured as she opened it.

The sheet, laid out in neat rows and columns, listed the name of each person who had vanished in Creston and the nearby area, the date they were first noted as missing, the names of their family members, and place of employment. This last was an eye-opener; all but one had worked at Sterling Enterprises, with a job title that sounded higher up than assembly-line worker. In a comments section, it was noted whether the rest of that person's family had subsequently moved away; several said: Left in the night.

"I'm impressed," Sam said, turning her screen so Beau could read it. "This guy is incredibly organized."

Cecelia circled the kitchen island to stand behind Beau and read over his shoulder. "Sterling. It's so obvious that's the common element." Her dark eyes met Sam's. "Why couldn't they have just taken Mark away and forced me to follow? I would have done it gladly." A tear slipped from the corner of her left eye.

# Chapter 9

Beau's pickup truck came to a stop in the visitors lot, in the shadow of the Sterling computer chip empire. They'd paused at the guard gate and been issued a parking permit. The sleek glass building towered above them, sunlight glinting off its surfaces, a beacon of modern-day success. Samantha peered up through the windshield, her eyes narrowing slightly as she took in the sight. "This is it," she said, popping the door open and stepping out onto the blacktop. "Seems a lot bigger up close."

"Fanciest thing I've ever seen here in Creston," Beau commented, joining her side and adjusting his hat against the glare. His casual drawl belied the sharpness in his gaze, already scanning for potential trouble spots.

They walked toward the entrance, Sam wondering what criminal activities might reach into the very heart of this corporation. And Cece's question last night still nagged at her. If others disappeared, why was Mark killed?

"Stop right there." The command came from a broad-shouldered security guard who stepped from behind a security desk, his hands held up in a clear gesture to halt their advance. He was in his forties and wore a crisp uniform, a stark contrast to Beau's jeans and Samantha's comfortable attire. "What time is your appointment and with whom?" he asked.

"We need to speak with Jason Blackwood," Beau told him. "Beau Cardwell and Samantha Sweet."

"Sorry folks," the guard continued after checking a list. His air of authority suggested he wouldn't budge easily. "Can't let you inside without an appointment."

Samantha exchanged a glance with Beau, her eyebrows raised. She offered the guard a smile warm enough to thaw a snowstorm. "We totally understand, but we're here on important business," she explained, her tone easygoing. "It's about the death of an employee, Mark Mitchell. Maybe you've heard about it?"

The guard's expression didn't change. "Everyone's heard, ma'am, but that doesn't mean I can let you waltz in. Company policy is strict."

"Can't you just call up to Mr. Blackwood's office?" Beau asked, his deep voice calm and friendly. He leaned slightly forward.

"We just want to help, is all."

"Your names aren't on the list. Can't help you," the guard replied, though now he seemed less certain, his stance relaxing just a fraction.

Beau sized up the guard, his years of law enforcement experience telling him that patience would win this standoff.

"We spoke yesterday with Chief Benson downtown, and the conversation raised a couple of questions." He pulled out his law enforcement ID and quickly flashed it toward the guard. "Really, only five minutes of Mr. Blackwood's time would clear it up and save us all a lot of time."

The guard hesitated, then reached for his radio and keyed the mic. He turned his back as he spoke softly into it.

Static crackled before a stern voice responded, "Let them through, but keep tabs on them."

Another guard approached and issued them visitor badges, watching as they clipped them on.

"Thank you kindly," Beau said, tipping his hat once more.

Samantha hid a grin as they walked past the security desk, her stride confident. "That went fairly well," she whispered.

"We haven't actually gotten to the man's office yet," Beau replied under his breath, eyes scanning the surroundings for any signs of trouble.

Their escort motioned for them to follow, and they stared at his ramrod straight back as they navigated a flight of stairs, then a maze of sterile hallways into a large open plan office.

"Stay sharp, Sam," Beau murmured. "These folks seem wound up."

Samantha caught snippets of hushed conversations as they passed cubicle after cubicle. Eyes peeked over monitors, following their every move. A silent alarm seemed to have swept through the space, setting everyone on edge. It was like walking into a beehive that had just been given a sharp tap.

"They must not get many visitors here," Samantha

murmured, her voice laced with humor.

Beau's gaze flitted through the place, never lingering.

The air felt thick with unspoken questions and curiosity. They pushed on, the carpet muffling their steps. Samantha noted the quick averted gazes, the abrupt end to phone calls as they approached. Someone even knocked over a coffee cup in a clumsy attempt to appear absorbed in work.

Beau's eyes narrowed slightly at the nervous employee.

They turned a corner, the corporate buzz fading behind them as they approached a large, imposing door. Beau raised an eyebrow at Samantha, "Showtime."

Their escort walked through the double doors, nodded to a secretary and told her Glasser had okayed the visit. She picked up a handset and pressed an intercom button. At her nod, the guard reached for the handle on the next set of doors. At a massive desk on the far side of the room sat Jason Blackwood, framed by the vast open countryside behind him. His silhouette, familiar from the pictures they'd seen, was all sharp angles and self-assured stillness. He didn't rise from his chair, simply steepled his fingers and regarded them with a look that could freeze mercury.

"Mr. and Mrs. Cardwell," Jason greeted, his voice smooth, almost welcoming. But his eyes, dark and calculating, belied his casual tone.

"Jason," Beau nodded, taking a step forward. Samantha followed, her senses tuned to the room's energy.

"Nice view you've got here," she said, with a nod toward the window.

"Comes with the territory," Jason replied, establishing a barely veiled display of dominance.

"Must be quite the territory," Beau observed, his voice steady.

They faced each other across the expanse of mahogany, Beau calm on the outside. Sam wondered if his gut was churning the way hers was. Her eyes locked on their host, reading the subtle shifts in his posture, the minute betrayals of tension in his otherwise polished facade. She wished she'd handled the magic box this morning, to get a better feel for his mood based on his aura.

"Please, sit," Jason invited. "Now, what can I do for you folks? Keeping in mind I have another appointment in less than five minutes." He held up a hand. "Maybe before dancing around the subject, I should just say that I get the impression you're here about … something to do with Mark Mitchell's unfortunate accident here on the property? If you're looking for an insurance settlement, you'll need to get in touch with our legal department."

"Insurance?" Beau chuckled softly, the sound as disarming as it was deliberate. "Is that what you think?" He pulled out his ID once more, although he had a feeling Blackwood already knew exactly who he was. "We're investigating what at the very least is a wrongful death, and at worst is a murder. I'm not after anything but the truth."

Jason leaned forward, his eyes narrowing. "You do realize that poking around in things you don't understand can be … unhealthy?"

"Is that a threat, Jason?" Samantha asked, her voice light, almost amused.

"Consider it friendly advice." Jason's lips curled into a semblance of a smile, but his eyes remained cold.

Beau's response was a slow nod, his own smile never reaching his eyes. "Your concern is touching, really. But your cooperation would be even better."

The smile coming across the desk took on an authentic

air. "Of course. I'm here to cooperate in every possible way. Please. Just let me know what, specifically, I can do."

"Someone in this company knows what happened to Mark. I believe someone in this company is directly responsible for his death and for the disappearances of several others. What you can do to help would be to open an internal investigation and to allow us and our investigator access to the records, the security footage of the parking garage, anything that could shed light on what really happened."

There was a beat of silence, electric and thick. Jason sat back in his chair, appraising them with a renewed interest. It was clear Beau had just laid out the terms of engagement, and neither he nor Samantha would be intimidated.

Jason made a placating gesture. "I can see how you might think those things would help, but believe me, the police went through all this. Sadly, Mr. Mitchell was attacked in a section of the garage where the cameras lack coverage. There was nothing useful there. And as for our employee records, what on earth would you hope to find? Someone with a history of attacking their fellow workers?" He chuckled. "Trust me, everyone hired here has gone through comprehensive background checks and has been vetted thoroughly for any criminal past. If they have such a past, they would never be hired at Sterling."

He stood, resting his fingertips on the shining surface of his desk. "Now, as I mentioned. I have another appointment."

"Good day, Mr. Blackwood," Beau said, standing up, his movement smooth and confident.

Samantha squared her shoulders, stepping into Jason's line of sight. "I'm certain, with enough digging and some help from law enforcement at a higher level than that here in Creston, we'll find the truth. It's out there."

Jason's smug grin faltered, and for a fleeting second, his mask slipped. Panic darted across his face like a shadow. But it was gone as quickly as it appeared, his trained composure snapping back into place.

"Accusations require proof, Samantha," he retorted with a forced chuckle, trying to regain his ground. "You have none. Now, may I walk you out?"

He stepped around the desk, buttoning his suit jacket, his arm extended to usher them through the open door.

Beau had seen the crack in the armor and knew they had hit a nerve. His lips quirked up in a half-smile as they traversed the corridor. At the elevator, Beau paused against the doorframe, a knowing gleam in his eye. "Evidence has a funny way of piling up when folks least expect it."

"Please," Jason sneered, waving a dismissive hand. "You're bluffing. You two are grasping at straws. I assure you, there is nothing to find here. Sterling and its employees were not involved in this sad incident. As Chief Benson must have surely told you, somehow an outsider got into the garage and lay in wait."

"There will be something. Photos. Emails. Testimonies." Beau's voice was calm, almost casual as he ticked off each point on his fingers. "Shall I go on?"

Jason paused, his eyes narrowing. "None of that exists. Please, folks, just go on back home and leave this. The authorities investigated and the case is solved."

The elevator doors whooshed open and Sam took Beau's arm to steer him inside. When they were alone, she whispered, "Did you notice, he used the same words as Benson. The case is solved."

"Later," Beau whispered, glancing upward where it would have been easy to conceal a camera or microphone.

Out in the truck, Beau drove away from the massive Sterling facility, eyeing his rearview mirrors as the guard at the door stood with arms crossed, watching them leave.

"That was weird," Sam said once they'd cleared the entry gates. "The employees were jittery as anything, didn't you think? And that Jason Blackwood—talk about running hot and cold. Pushy then friendly, cooperative without actually saying anything?"

Beau nodded but remained quiet. Two miles down the highway, he pulled into the parking lot of a farm supply store and stopped next to a white pickup. He got out, walked along the side of his truck and stooped next to the rear tire.

Sam joined him. "Beau, what are you—" Her mouth snapped shut as she watched him pull a tiny device from under the wheel well.

"A tracker."

# Chapter 10

Beau pivoted to the white truck beside him and clicked the magnetic device in place on the other vehicle. "There now," he said, dusting off his hands. "Whoever's monitoring this thing will go away in a whole other direction. Even if they somehow have camera surveillance connected to it, they'll just see a white truck of the same make and model as mine."

"Wow," Sam said as they took their seats again. "How did you know?"

"I didn't. But those security guys at Sterling weren't your normal rent-a-cop types, and I overheard a comment when they called up to Blackwood's office. We can't forget we're dealing with people who are at the top of the high-tech game."

"You didn't trust a word he said, did you?"

Beau started his truck and pulled out of the parking lot. "Everything he dropped, about how caring they were toward their employees, how thorough the investigation was … total bull."

"I thought there was maybe one true snippet in there. I got the feeling that trust is a pretty rare commodity inside that company. Almost like Jason was feeding us a hint. Or maybe he inadvertently let it slip."

Beau nodded thoughtfully. "You could be right. I'd lean toward an accidental slip, though. I do not, for a moment, believe that guy is out to help us."

"What about Olivia Sterling, the CEO? I wish we'd had a chance to talk with her."

"Agreed. We'll see if we can make that happen. It'd be nice if we caught her outside the office. I definitely have the impression everyone there is looking over their shoulder at all times."

"You think? Even the boss?"

He shrugged, slowing as they reached the center of town. "You up for some lunch?"

"Yeah, sounds good. Should we call Cecelia?" Sam reached for her phone. "I'd hate to mess up plans she might have." She tapped the number in her contact list.

"Ooh, lunch out sounds good to me. You know where's a good place, if y'all like Chinese?" She didn't pause for an answer. "Golden Palace. It's on Second, kinda behind the veterinarian's office. It's early enough that we'll beat the crowd."

Sam gave Beau a blank look. "I'm sure we'll find it," he said. "Ten minutes?"

"Five. I'm hungry." She laughed and ended the call.

By the time Cecelia bustled into the small restaurant

and greeted the owner by name, Beau and Sam had a table and a pot of jasmine tea between them. Beau had pulled out his little notebook and was jotting down the basics about their visit to Sterling Enterprises this morning, his brow furrowed in concentration.

Sam paused in pouring three tiny cups of the fragrant tea and greeted Cece.

"If y'all haven't ordered yet, I can recommend the buffet. Course that's because I love trying a little of everything." She draped her light jacket over the back of the chair across from Sam's.

"I'll walk up there with you," Sam said. "He's a little occupied."

The ladies loaded their plates and carried them back to the table, where Beau was still scribbling notes about the various interviews.

"Sam," Beau started, not looking up from his notebook. "We need more information from people we can trust."

Sam's mind raced through the faces they'd encountered, each one a piece of the puzzle.

Cecelia chimed in. "You talked to Lucy Evergreen," she began, tapping her finger on the table. "She knows this community inside out."

"True," Beau nodded. "She's known everyone here forever, and I sensed she has good instincts about them."

"Don't forget Aiden Wilder." Samantha's voice held a note of respect. "PI skills, plus he's got that charm to get people talking. We should check back in with him. And Ethan Hawthorne, the librarian. He's got knowledge we don't even know we need yet."

"Quiet guy," Beau murmured, recalling Ethan's unassuming presence. "But sharp. His brain could crack codes we haven't seen."

"Plus, he's got this … steadiness," Samantha added. "Feels like he'd have our backs."

Cecelia nodded at that. "Our biggest problem right now is that we don't know what questions to ask."

"It's always that way when a new case comes along. But you just keep plugging away at it," Beau said, his tone shifting as resolve set in. "And that's what we'll do."

He walked to the buffet and made his choices, heavy on the spring rolls, Sam noted.

"I want to talk with Aiden again," he said as he dipped the first of the rolls in sweet and sour sauce. "Now that we've looked at his spreadsheet, it would be a good time to compare notes."

Cecelia wiped her fingers on her napkin. "You're welcome to look through Mark's desk at home. I doubt there's anything there. The police took his laptop for a while and returned it."

"So, if there was anything relevant, I'd bet it's gone now," Sam said.

"Yeah, the chief stonewaller, Benson, would have kept it if there was anything he needed," Beau added.

"Or wiped the hard drive," Sam suggested. "Have you turned the computer on since he gave it back?"

Cece shook her head. "No, actually. I have my own, for my charity files and all that."

"What types of things did Mark do with his?"

"Oh, you know. Watched movies in the evenings. Researched any little subject that interested him. Shopped on Amazon." She laughed, but Beau remained thoughtful.

"I'd like to take a look at his, once we're back at the house," he said.

Sam gave him a sideways look. "Maybe we should have Aiden do that." She placed a hand on his arm. "Not that you aren't brilliant, honey, but computers aren't exactly your strong point."

He gave a rueful grin and stabbed a forkful of broccoli.

"Mark didn't bring home any company records at all," Cece clarified. "It was strictly forbidden."

And yet, Sam thought, she already admitted that Mark didn't talk about his work so how would Cece know what he may have brought home? She kept that to herself.

"I'll give you access to everything—Mark's office, his documents, his computer. Whatever it takes. I should have shared that information before."

"I should have thought to ask for it earlier. Are you going right home after this?" The last bite of spring roll popped into his mouth.

"I've got one quick stop, then yes. I need to be home by one. A friend is stopping over, a young gal who's on the board of a kids charity with me."

"Can you gather up Mark's computer and stuff, have it ready for us? We can keep to another room so we don't disturb your meeting."

"You can have his study all to yourselves," she said, standing and gathering her purse and jacket. "See you in a while."

"I feel like we should get Aiden's take on our visit to Sterling Microchips this morning," Sam said, once they were alone again. "What do you think?"

"We'll have more to discuss if we go through Mark's belongings first. Let's do that, then we can reach out to Aiden later in the afternoon."

"Good plan."

They arrived at Cece's house before their hostess, and quickly scouted around enough to locate Mark's home office. It was a functional room with enough personal memorabilia on display that Sam guessed the decorator had minimal input here.

A large desk sat in front of a wall of trophies—a deer head, two stuffed trout and one lake bass. So Mark the accountant had an outdoorsy side as well. More predictably, a credenza held files with labels denoting personal bills paid, mortgage papers, tax returns, and statements from an investment portfolio. She noted that the cabinet was freely accessible and thought she should recommend to Cece that she keep it locked.

A large, flat screen TV was mounted to the wall in front of the desk, and two comfy chairs could be swiveled toward the television or toward the desk. Although the home was large enough for, and Cece had hinted at, a home theater, gym, and game room, Sam commented to Beau that this room looked like the one where Mark spent a lot of his free time.

"Hey you guys," came Cecelia's voice from the doorway, "did you find the computer?"

The top of the desk held office supplies and a few knickknacks, but no computer.

"We hadn't actually taken the time to look yet," Sam replied.

"It's right over here," Cece said, reaching for a soft-sided computer bag that leaned against one wall. She picked it up and set it on the desk, just as the doorbell rang. "And there's my meeting. Have fun."

Sam opened the bag and set up the computer, plugging it into a power strip below the desk and booting it up.

Softly closing the door, Beau began a systematic check of the room, beginning by pulling out each desk drawer and looking at the underside.

"Interesting." He reached into his shirt pocket and pulled out his little notebook, jotting a series of numbers. "Looks to me like the combination to a safe. We'll have to ask Cece where that is."

In one of the side drawers, he found a sheaf of bank statements for a joint checking account. "Might want to look through these. Mark must have had an old-man streak. He had the bank send paper statements with images of the checks."

Sam laughed at his description, but he was right. She didn't know anyone in their age group who hadn't done their banking online for a couple decades now. "It feels kind of creepy to go through them," she said, setting the pages aside. "Let's wait until your cousin can review them first."

"What does the computer tell us?"

"Let's see …" Sam went straight to the hard drive and began searching.

The word Sterling brought several results, but none suspicious, mostly documents in which Mark merely mentioned his employer's name. His email account wasn't locked, so she performed a similar search there, with no matches at all. Keying in the names they knew, Olivia Sterling and Jason Blackwood, came up again with zero matches.

"I think that's more telling than if there had been a dozen matches. Who doesn't mention their boss's name in an email to a friend, at least once in a while?" she commented. "Kind of goes along with our supposition that

Chief Benson's department tampered with the computer while it was in their possession."

"We can't say that for sure, Sam. But yeah, I find it suspicious." He closed another of the drawers and stood up straight, rubbing his back. "What about searching for the names of some of those disappearances? We know most of them were employed at the same place."

"Ooh, great idea. I'll grab my laptop and get Aiden's spreadsheet."

Sam walked out of the first-floor study and headed toward the stairs, but heard her name coming from the kitchen. She peered around the corner.

"Sam, I want you and Beau to meet Melissa Fields, my right hand when it comes to our committee on the hospital charity board."

Sam stepped into the room, where the two women had papers and a couple of colorful posters spread on the kitchen island. Melissa had raven hair, shoulder length, and was a few years younger, probably in her early forties. Her warm smile lit up when Sam greeted her.

"Happy to meet you. Beau's in the study, Cece. Shall I get him?"

"Oh, we'll catch him later." Cece turned to Melissa. "I don't know if I mentioned that Beau is my cousin and Sam is his wife. Beau was sheriff of Taos County, in New Mexico, and I asked them here to see if we can find the real truth about Mark's death."

Melissa's face crumpled, echoing her friend's pain. "It was so awful, him dying that way. And there's not a one of us who believes what the police chief says." She held up a hand. "I'm sorry, but there is no love lost when it comes to that man Benson."

"In other words, Sam, you may speak freely in front of Melissa." Cecelia's smile was the most genuine Sam had seen since their arrival.

"So, you knew Mark as well?"

Melissa nodded. "I guess. Seeing as how I'd helped set his broken bone and patch up his face after that beating."

# Chapter 11

"What? What beating?" Sam felt her mouth hanging open.

"Oh, right. I guess I didn't mention that Mark had a previous altercation at work," Cecelia said, shuffling a little. "Details at ten, if you really want them."

Melissa took up the slack. "I'm a nurse at the hospital. It's where I first met these two. Mark came into our ER with those injuries and I was on duty that night. Anyway …" she turned to Cece and patted her shoulder "… we became good friends and started working on some committees together."

Sam could tell Melissa was respecting Cece's desire not to go into the full story here and now, so she did the same. "Well, I was just on my way up to our room for something. It was nice meeting you, Melissa. Maybe we'll catch up again at some point."

She fled the kitchen, in time to hear Cece give a long sigh.

Back in the study, she found Beau sitting in one of the leather chairs, going through a little stack of handwritten notes on various scraps of paper. She set up her computer and found the spreadsheet with Aiden's list of the missing people. One by one, she entered names into a search on Mark's computer. Only two of them resulted in matches, both of those in emails more than two years old. She made a note of those names.

"Hon, can I ask you a question?"

Beau looked up.

"Have you come across either of these names—Bill Lakman or Hanu Chen?"

"No, why?"

"Seems Mark sent emails with some work-related question, but neither replied to him. The email thread went cold. Then each of those men went missing." A shiver went down her spine as she voiced the truth.

Beau's expression got serious for a full minute. "That seems significant. Were there others from the missing-list, people Mark tried to contact?"

Sam shrugged. "Those are the only two I found. Keep in mind this is his personal computer. We'll probably never know what was on his computer at work. The email Mark sent these two is pretty cryptic but it sounds like he's telling them not to respond at work, to keep the correspondence personal."

"And you think the police missed these in their search, doing whatever they did to Mark's computer while it was in their custody?"

"I have no idea. But most likely, yes." She picked up

a pen and tapped it nervously on the notepad beside her. "Have you been through all the files in this credenza, Beau?"

"Some, not all. Why?"

"Just now, when I went up to get my computer …" she dropped her voice "… I met a nurse, Cece's friend Melissa, who's here for their meeting. She let it drop that she once treated Mark for a broken bone and other effects of a beating. I wonder if there are health records."

She turned the desk chair around and reached for one of the drawers.

"Cece never mentioned that to us," Beau said.

"I know. And she didn't really seem to want to talk about it now. Could be she was getting impatient to get back to the business of the charity. But I thought we might ask more about that when we're alone with her. She did use the words 'altercation at work'."

"More indication that whatever got Mark targeted had to do with his job."

"Beau? Do you get the feeling Cece is holding back, not sharing everything? I mean, this is only one thing. Could there be more?"

"It's worth noting, but don't read too much into it, Sam. We've only been here a couple of days. We really can't expect that she would pour out all her troubles—past and present—right away."

She sent him a warm smile. "You're right."

He went back to the notes in his hands and she closed the drawer and returned to her computer searches. But there were still questions in her mind. What was the real story here, anyway?

None of the other missing persons' names showed up

on Mark's computer, so Sam gave up that tactic in favor of flipping through files in the credenza. Most of those turned out to be standard personal files—paid bills, travel plans, and other things she felt were not her business and probably not related to their case. She'd pulled out a checkbook and spare check register and set them aside when a tap came at the door.

"Hey, guys," Cecelia said, sticking her head around the edge when she opened it. "Am I interrupting?"

Sam laughed. "It's your home. If anything, we're the ones creating chaos here."

"Melissa and I finished our meeting and I thought I'd see if y'all need anything. Can I bring you an iced tea?" She checked her watch. "Heck, it's already getting late. We could declare it time for happy hour if you want."

"I think we've got a couple of questions," Sam said, reaching for the check register. "If you could flip through this whenever you have time, and let me know if there's anything that seems unusual or unexplained?"

Beau stacked the pages he'd been looking at and reached for his notebook. "I spotted some numbers that look like they might belong to a safe. Can you show me that?"

"Sure. I doubt you would have found it on your own." She stepped into the room and walked over to a large painting on the wall. "This was one of those cool features Mark insisted we add to the house."

Sam and Beau exchanged a look behind her back. Seriously, they wouldn't have thought to look behind a painting for a wall safe?

But when Cece moved the painting aside, the wall behind it appeared blank. Then, somewhere along the frame of the picture, she pressed a hidden button and a panel in the wall slid silently aside. She entered the code and the small door flipped open.

Inside were a couple of bundles of cash. "Mark's rainy day money," she said with a snicker. "And let's see … my jewelry organizers, our passports, marriage license, birth certificates … and hmm. Not sure what this little book is. Mark loved to keep little ledgers—the accountant in him, I guess. He'd track expenses and other stuff, handwritten as backup to the computer. I'm surprised you didn't come across all that in the other files."

"Mind if I look?" Beau asked, accepting the small journal when she handed it to him. He settled back into the leather chair and opened the book.

Cecelia picked up the check registers Sam had left on the corner of the desk. "How far back should I look?"

"I don't know," Sam said. "Start with the most recent entries and go back through it?"

Beau nodded, not taking his eyes off the journal in his hand. As the other two settled in with their tasks, Sam felt a little at loose ends and wandered into the kitchen. A familiar feeling stirred inside her, back to her days as a young mother when she felt stressed and would turn to baking as an outlet.

She shook her head, rationalizing that she didn't feel especially stressed right now. But her feet carried her to the pantry and her eyes scanned the shelves. Flour—check. Sugar—check. Some canned pumpkin, a few spices, and she was ready. Twenty minutes later, the first sheet of her special pumpkin spice cookies was coming out of the oven. As the second batch baked, she found cream cheese in the fridge and stirred up a bowl of frosting for them.

"What's that heavenly smell?" Cecelia exclaimed,

drifting into the kitchen, her approach silent in her socks.

Sam held out the cooling rack. "Sorry to make a mess in here. It was a spur-of-the-moment idea."

Cece took one of the soft cookies and her eyes rolled in pleasure. "Sam, these are fantastic. Wow."

"It's a pretty easy recipe, and you happened to have everything on hand."

"I'm surprised. I'm really not much of a baker. I guess Mark's sister left some things on hand after last Christmas."

Sam eyed the item Cece had set on the counter. "Did you find something?"

"Not much," she mumbled through cookie crumbs. Swallowing, she picked up the check register and flipped it open. "You suggested I look for anything unusual, and I only came across one thing that didn't make sense to me."

She turned sideways and held the booklet so Sam could take a look.

"This entry, a check for a thousand dollars made out to Cash. And when I looked up the image of the check in the bank statements, the notation only says JCI." She looked up, her brow wrinkled. "I have no idea who or what that is. And why on earth would he need to cash a check for it?"

"Did you show this to Beau?"

"Yes. He hadn't come across anything that would match a JCI in that little journal. At least not yet."

Beau walked into the kitchen just then, and Sam asked about the JCI notation. He nodded as he reached for two of the pumpkin cookies. "I found one note, and it doesn't tell me much of anything. But JCI, whoever or whatever that is, gave Mark some crucial information. He has a note beside the name—Eureka! This was about three weeks before he died."

# Chapter 12

Cecelia swallowed hard and looked a little queasy. Sam glanced toward the clock on the microwave and saw it was beyond dinnertime.

"Let's get some solid food in us. We'll think more clearly," she suggested. "I spotted a take-and-bake pizza in the fridge. Since the oven's hot already, should I just put that—?"

Cece nodded and sank onto one of the stools at the counter. "Eureka. It's what Mark always said when he'd solved a problem, anything from getting the lawn mower started to balancing an especially tricky accounting entry."

Sam turned toward the others after putting the pizza in the oven. "So, how do these things tie together? Beau, you said the comment in the journal was written about three weeks before Mark died. Was that near the time he was threatened and beaten?"

He shook his head. "That was a couple months before any of this."

Cecelia reached for the bottle of wine they'd opened last night, and she gestured for Sam to bring glasses. Sam took the bottle and poured each of them a small one, while Beau found a beer in the fridge. Faces were solemn as they clinked their glasses.

"Cece, do you feel like talking about that beating? Maybe there's some detail that would be helpful as we start questioning other people."

She sighed and ran her finger along the rim of her wine glass. "It was pretty much what Melissa said—he had a broken collarbone and a lot of bruises. I was afraid he might lose one eye, it was so badly bruised."

"Do you know what led to the attack?" Beau asked. "I think you said he wasn't robbed, so it sounds like the motive was anger or perhaps revenge. Did he share anything about that?"

"When we got home from the ER, he only said, 'Looks like I poked the right bear.' Mostly he was under the influence of all the painkillers they gave him, so he went right to bed."

"Poked the right bear ... so he really was onto something. Something at work."

She nodded as the oven timer dinged.

"Who was he investigating? Or maybe it was some procedure at the office that he took exception to?"

"I'm not sure, Beau. Like I said, he didn't share a lot about his work there. I always thought it was because of all those NDAs, but maybe he knew it was dangerous and was keeping me safe."

"Understandable," he said as Sam brought out plates

and served slices of the veggie pizza. "But now we need to think. Anything he said could be helpful."

"Well, I know he talked to the police, after the beating. I guess someone at the hospital reported it, or maybe some bystander who saw what bad shape he was in. They came here the day after the ER visit and asked questions. Mark wasn't one to fudge the facts by saying he fell down the stairs or something. He plainly told them he was beaten up right outside his place of work."

"What did they do?"

"Nothing." Cece took another swallow of her wine, shrugging. "So, okay, in fairness he didn't name his attacker. They pressed that question and he said he hadn't seen them clearly. That part, I knew, was not true. He was scared."

"Did you ask him later, after the police had left?" Sam asked.

"I did. Mark told me to back off. I was better off not knowing."

Beau tapped the cover of the journal he'd been studying. "Nearly all his entries here are coded somehow. Where it concerns people—I'm guessing—he used initials. But some of those could be businesses, as well."

"Such as that JCI reference from the check?"

"Possibly." He turned back to Cece. "Was there anyplace else he did his research, maybe another computer that he hid away somewhere?"

"No, I'm ninety-nine percent sure he had no other computer. Mark could keep a secret but he wasn't secretive. Does that make sense? I mean, if he'd had a girlfriend on the side or rented a secret storage unit or something, I'd have figured that out. With me, he was an open book except for his work at Sterling. It was the one subject he kept separate from our family life."

"Okay." Beau finished his slice and took a second one. "But if you think of anything else …"

Cece held up her index finger. "There could be … It just hit me. He spent a lot of time at the library. In this day and age, when you can do all kinds of research from your own computer …"

"Maybe he was using the public computers to perform searches he wouldn't want traced to either his personal or work computers," Sam said. "Cece, that makes a lot of sense."

She turned to Beau. "We should talk to Ethan Hawthorne again. Maybe he'll know something."

"I could use help from someone with a knowledge of accounting, as well," Beau said. "If Mark was uncovering irregularities in the way the books are kept out at Sterling, his notes in the journal probably pertain to that. But I don't know accountant-speak well enough to decipher them."

"Maybe Aiden?" Sam suggested.

"Lucy Evergreen," Cecelia said.

"The high school teacher? Really?"

"She teaches several subjects, and one of them is basic accounting," Cece told them. "I don't know how deep her knowledge goes, but she could point you in the right direction if she doesn't know the answers."

"This is good," Beau said. "It's progress. So, Sam, how about if you go to the library tomorrow and talk to Ethan. I'll see what I can learn if I show a couple of these journal entries to Lucy. We'll make progress quicker if we split up."

"Um, truck?" Sam gave him a straight look.

"You need two vehicles," Cece said. "I've got a couple of spares." She rose and led the way through the pantry and laundry room to the connecting garage. Flipping the light switch, she waved her arm toward the three stalls.

There stood a sedan, an SUV, and a gleaming sports car.

"I normally drive my little Lexus there, but you're welcome to either of the others."

Sam told her she'd be far more at ease in the gray Toyota 4-Runner than the Corvette. "I imagine that bright red speedster is known all over town," she said with a laugh.

"Well, yeah. It was Mark's midlife-crisis car, and he did love zipping up and down the highway in it. Plus, it was the one he often drove to work."

"Then, for sure, the Toyota it is."

Cecelia yawned as she turned out the garage light.

"This has been a long day for you," Sam said. "Why don't you go on to bed? Beau and I can clean up the kitchen."

"I probably won't sleep; I almost never do, these days. But thank you. I'll take you up on the offer."

They watched his cousin head for her rooms on the other side of the house, her feet shuffling a little. "I feel so sorry for her," Sam said. "I don't know what I'd do, in her place, if something happened to you." It nearly had. She shook off the memory of Beau's close call a few years ago.

He pulled her close and she pressed her face to his chest. "We've got a lot of years yet, honey. Let's don't be thinking about any other scenario."

Sam had a feeling Mark would have said the same thing to his wife. And look how that turned out.

# Chapter 13

Beau was awake at daybreak, stirring softly and trying not to wake Sam as he slid out of the king-size bed in their room. He showered and dressed quickly, making his way downstairs for a cup of coffee and a piece of toast. The rest of the house was quiet as he left.

He made the five-minute drive to the high school, parking in the near-empty faculty lot, sipping the coffee from his travel mug. He hoped Lucy Evergreen was one who arrived early to prep for her classes, that he might get the chance to speak with her and get her opinion about some of the cryptic journal entries before she began her teaching day. Otherwise, he would probably have to wait until she got a lunch break or free period.

One by one, vehicles began arriving. Teachers emerged and headed toward the admin offices, presumably to pick up messages before heading to their classrooms. Beau watched, hoping he would recognize Lucy, considering he'd seen her only once. Sometimes, he felt his law enforcement skills were slipping from lack of practice.

Then she arrived, driving a practical Subaru, dark blue in color. Her graying hair was styled in the same chin-length bob, and her slender build was instantly recognizable as she stepped from the driver's seat. He got out of his truck, making sure he closed the door with a loud thud, letting his bootsteps echo on the pavement, so as not to let her think he was sneaking up.

"Hello, Lucy," he greeted, tipping his Stetson.

"Sheriff Cardwell. Nice to see you again."

He smiled, admiring her memory for faces. Then again, he was one of the few strangers in town right now. He might be more memorable than he wanted to be.

"I'm still looking into Mark Mitchell's case and wonder if I might trouble you for a few minutes before your classes begin."

She shifted her purse strap to the other shoulder and set her briefcase on the ground beside the car door. "How can I help?"

He pulled Mark's journal from his inner coat pocket and opened it to a page he'd dogeared. "I understand you have some background in bookkeeping or accounting. I wonder if these lines mean anything, in that context." His finger traced two lines of writing that he'd assumed were accounting related.

"Oh my. I'm not really sure. Guess I need to get my head into that world again. May I take this book with me and study it a little?"

"I really can't let it go. It's a one-of-a-kind thing."

She met his gaze. "I understand." Seeing his disappointment, she came up with an idea. "My first period class has a test today. I can get my assistant to monitor them, and maybe we could go into the teacher's lounge for a look at this, once I get them started."

"That's perfect," he said.

"Walk along with me and I'll show you where to wait. There'll be some announcements and such, but I'll be free in fifteen minutes or so. Does that work for you?"

She led the way into the building, let the office administrator know his presence was fine, and took him into a lounge where a half-dozen people were holding coffee mugs and chatting. The ringing of an old-fashioned school bell took Beau back a bunch of years; it also worked to disperse the crowd. Lucy mouthed 'be right back' and headed out with the rest of them.

Never good at waiting in an empty room, Beau decided to use the time to put in a call to Aiden Wilder and see if he could set up a meeting with the private investigator. He pulled out his phone but the call went to voicemail. He left a short message, suggesting they meet anytime after mid-morning.

A male voice droned over the school's speaker system; the principal, he guessed, giving the morning announcements. Another blast from the past, Beau thought with a smile. Five minutes later, Lucy Evergreen walked back into the lounge.

"All right. I've got thirty or forty minutes." She headed straight to the coffee machine, but found the carafe only held sludge at the bottom.

"I can get you—"

"Never mind. I had two at home and don't need

another one," she said with a laugh. "Now—about those entries in the book?"

She took another chair near his and he handed over the journal, open to the page he had in mind. She puzzled over it silently for a couple of minutes.

"Some of these look like accounting terms. The letters 'cr' mean a credit, 'dr' is a debit. Or sometimes a credit is designated with brackets. The writer of this seemed to use those at times too, brackets around a set of numbers."

"Do you have any idea what they mean?"

"Not a clue. They're just numbers to anyone who doesn't know what they refer to." She slid her finger over to the facing page. "Now, some of this is more like business terminology. BOL often stands for Bill of Lading, which would be a document listing items within a shipment. COD usually refers to receiving payment upon delivery. They could, of course, have different meanings within a particular company. Every business seems to develop its own form of a language. And don't even get me started on the government. Contracts with government agencies often read like an alphabet soup of made-up words."

"Let me make a list of the most common terms an accountant would use. I can see I'll need to go back through this with more knowledge."

Lucy pulled out a sheet of plain paper and jotted down a short list: TJ = Transaction Journal; GJ = General Journal; SJ = Sales Journal. He was getting the idea. If it included a J, there was probably a corresponding entry in a journal of some kind. Along with the shorthand entries she'd mentioned earlier, he might be able to pull together something with meaning. Clearly, he would need more information about Sterling Enterprises and their overall operations before much of it would make sense.

"Lucy, thank you so much," he said when she slid the list over to him. "I must say, I really admire your attention to detail."

She blushed a little. "My students complain that I'm too detail oriented. That it's my superpower to use when I'm grading their tests."

"Hey, it's not a bad superpower to have."

"Speaking of tests …"

"Yes, I need to let you go back to your class. Again, thanks." He was halfway across the parking lot when his phone rang. Aiden Wilder's number showed on the screen.

"Hey man, what's up?" the PI greeted.

"Wondering if you've got time to get together? I've got a journal that needs interpretation, and I just got some good keys for doing that."

A pause. "I'm following a lead on one of those people who vanished," Aiden said. "The wife worked at Sterling. They've since relocated to Amarillo. I'm on my way there now. Should be home by tonight."

"Call me when you get back to Creston. If it's not too late maybe we can get together. Otherwise, tomorrow's good."

"Excellent. Maybe by then you'll have a translation of that journal you mentioned."

Maybe. Beau unlocked his truck and got in. He didn't hold a lot of hope that he could make sense of the little book that weighed heavily in his pocket right now.

# Chapter 14

Sam heard Beau's truck leave and watched from the bedroom window as he turned the corner. She was not in such a hurry to drop by the library. It didn't open until nine, and she wanted to give Ethan a little time to settle into his day before she popped in. Hearing sounds from the kitchen and the scent of coffee wafting up, she pulled on her robe and padded down the stairs to see what Cecelia was up to.

Cece greeted her with a bright smile as she pulled a mug from the cupboard for Sam. "I'm assuming you want coffee?"

Sam gave a nod. "You doing better today?"

"Oh, yeah. This grieving process … it's really weird. I feel pretty good, moving through my days, then I'll have a spell like yesterday where I can't drag myself off the couch."

Sam reached out and placed a hand on her shoulder.

"It helps a lot that you and Beau are here." The coffee machine sputtered at the end of its cycle and Cece handed Sam her mug.

"I hope we'll find something useful. So far, it seems we've hit a lot of dead ends." Sam took her mug and sat at the counter. "You haven't come up with what the initials JCI might stand for, have you?"

"That checkbook entry? No. I can think of a few friends whose first names start with J, but the rest doesn't match. And I can't think of a single reason any of those friends would need a thousand-dollar loan."

"The letter I at the end could stand for Incorporated. Maybe JCI is a company?"

"None that I'm familiar with. I suppose Mark could have bought something, but usually he'd mention it to me for a purchase that large. And why use cash?" Cece shrugged and turned toward the pantry. "Would you like a croissant? I bought some fresh, yesterday."

As the pastries warmed and Cece refilled their coffees, Sam thought about what she might ask Ethan when she got to the library.

"I've got another committee meeting today, Sam. You're welcome to tag along if you want to. This is the arts council, and the big topic is our upcoming Christmas bazaar. Handing out booth assignments is like walking on political eggshells. Some of the artists are, let's say, fragile of temperament."

Sam chuckled at the description. "I'll pass. I'm hoping the library will give me some clues to the questions we couldn't answer in Mark's journal yesterday. After that, I'm not sure. I'll see what Beau's up to and we might grab some lunch out."

"I gotta say I don't blame you a bit. Committee meetings aren't exactly entertaining." Cece put two croissants on a plate for Sam, another for herself, then set out butter and jam.

Sam bit in, savoring the flavors, although her own pastries at Sweet's Sweets were flakier. She kept that opinion to herself. She had to admit she was missing home and her own environment, hoping this case in Oklahoma would wrap up quickly.

Thirty minutes later, she'd showered and was choosing a blue pullover and black slacks from the closet. Running her fingers through her damp hair, she applied product to give it some body, and did her minimal makeup routine of blusher and lip gloss. She spotted the carved box where she'd set it on the dresser and decided to fortify herself with its energy. As she held the box in her hands, the dark wood began to warm and glow to a golden color.

She picked up the keys Cece had handed her last night, and went downstairs and out to the garage where the Toyota waited for her. Cece's Lexus was already gone. She located the button to open the garage door and then sat in the SUV, familiarizing herself with the controls and all the extra electronic gear, which was way more modern than that in her own truck or bakery delivery van.

She was on the streets of Creston five minutes later, remembering the route to the library. Ethan was deep in the stacks, peeping around the edge of a section of fiction when she walked in.

"I'm Samantha Sweet—we met yesterday …" she said, making sure the door closed softly behind her.

"Yes. I remember." He stepped out into the aisle, setting an armful of books on a cart. "Can I help you find something?"

"I hope so, but it's not a particular book, mainly questions. Do you have a minute?"

"Sure." He certainly wasn't a gregarious sort, she reflected. Then again, she remembered what Cece had said about Ethan's innate shyness.

"My husband mentioned that we're looking into the death of Mark Mitchell. Did Mark ever come in here and use the public computers?"

Ethan adjusted his glasses; his unkempt brown hair seemed fuzzier than before. "Occasionally, yes."

"I don't suppose you'd know what type of work he was doing here?"

"Searches, I gathered. The first time he came in he didn't seem familiar with the browser that comes as the default on our system." He walked over to one of the computers and moved the mouse to wake it up.

Sam didn't recognize the page either.

"But he got the hang of it quickly."

"Would there be any possibility that his browsing history would still be here?"

"Oh, no. I mean, I seriously doubt it. We encourage our patrons not to save passwords on these computers and to save their work to an external drive of some type, like a flash drive or something. It's really for their own security."

"I understand. And you're fairly certain Mark did this each time he visited?"

"I would bet on it. There was something … I don't know … secretive about whatever he was working on."

Sam began to pay attention to the faint aura she could see around Ethan's form. Sometimes the carved box gave her this ability, and she'd found that the stronger a person's emotions, the brighter the aura. If someone was being deceptive, the aura would grow in size and intensity. Ethan's seemed fairly neutral and she believed he was telling the truth. She decided to push a little further.

"Secretive … in what way? Do you think it had something to do with his job?"

He hesitated for a long moment. "I have no idea. As I say, I don't watch over people's shoulders when they're in here."

That had a faint, very faint, ring of untruth and she wondered whether there were times Ethan sneaked a peek. She let it drop, for the moment.

"We came across a notation that Cecelia couldn't identify, a reference to a JCI. Any idea what that stands for?"

His focus shifted to somewhere in the middle of the room. "No, I don't think I've ever heard it before."

"Could we look? Maybe choose the computer Mark most often used and see if anything points toward that reference?"

She knew he could see where she was going with this, and his interest quickly picked up. "Sure, let's give it a try." He pointed toward the terminal at the far left-hand end of the long desk. "Do you want to key in the words, or shall I?" he asked.

"Would you? You're familiar with the system and would be much quicker at it."

He took the chair, activated the browser, and turned to her. "It was J-C-I, right?"

She nodded and watched as his fingers flew over the keys. The screen immediately returned several results: a JCI Industries in Germany, makers of glass for auto windshields; the Judicial Court of Iowa; and Jews Concerned with Injustice. None of those felt quite right for her purposes.

"None of those came up in the browser bar by default," Ethan said, "so they haven't turned up in a search here. I'll try JCI dot com."

Nothing. Similarly with the other familiar possibilities such as dot gov, dot org, or dot net.

"Maybe those are the initials of a person," she suggested. "Is there a way to search for that?"

"Not any way that's practical. If the last name begins with an I, I maybe be able to come up with some possibilities among Oklahoma residents. We also have old telephone directories for that."

"This is a case where the phone book sounds faster," Sam commented. "Point me toward them."

He rose and led her to a corner shelf unit where there were, literally, huge stacks of directories. "Unless you have a better idea, I'd start with the closest, geographically, and work my way outward." He pointed toward one stack that was all Oklahoma books, with Creston on top of the pile.

"Good plan."

"Understand, most of these are quite dated. The phone companies have all but stopped issuing printed directories these days."

Ethan went back to the computer terminal. Sam carried the books for Creston, Enid, and Oklahoma City to a nearby table and plopped into a chair beside them. As he'd predicted, finding a person's name with the initials JCI went quickly. Few surnames began with an I, and fewer with a first name starting with a J. Within ten minutes she'd jotted down a half-dozen possibilities, along with their addresses and phone numbers.

Searching the yellow pages for businesses was far

trickier, as they were listed by category and she had absolutely nothing to go on. She returned the phone books to their place and joined Ethan at the computer desk.

His search had returned a few business names, which he'd dutifully copied and pasted into a document along with links to websites. "I can follow through on these, but since I don't know what type of business would relate in some way to Mark and his activities, I don't know that it'll be much help."

"Whatever you can do would be much appreciated," she told him. "But don't devote a lot of time to it. We could just be shouting up a flagpole here."

"I can call you or Cecelia if I find anything," he said. For the first time, a timid smile crossed his features.

She thanked him, pocketed her little handwritten list of names, and walked out to her ride. A glance at the clock told her it was well after eleven. She sent Beau a quick text, asking if he'd like to meet up for lunch somewhere. He wasn't normally the quickest at responding to texts, so she started driving toward the center of town, eyes alert for something appealing. When she spotted a cute tearoom that seemed bustling already, she pulled to the curb.

Beau's response came through: Sure, where?

She gave him the name of the place and said she'd grab a table. Then she wondered if the big, handsome sheriff of Taos County would be agreeable to tearoom fare. She stepped to the sidewalk and checked out the menu on a chalkboard there. The shepherd's pie or the hearty beef stew ought to be to his liking, she decided, and if not they would simply go somewhere else.

Sam stepped inside, hoping the lacy curtains and predominance of female customers wouldn't be off-putting, but the scents of beef, pastry, and complex combinations of herbs allayed those fears. She was shown to a corner table for four and told the hostess she would wait until her husband arrived before ordering.

Beau was there within five minutes and he strolled across the room without blinking an eye. The majority of the women in the room were also unblinking, only losing interest when he walked up to Sam's table and kissed her. He hung his Stetson on a nearby rack and took a seat across from Sam.

Once they'd placed their orders—shepherd's pie for him, a chicken salad sandwich for her—they compared notes from their morning interviews. He pulled out the list of accounting terms Lucy had shared with him. "Guess I'll go back through Mark's journal this afternoon and see if this helps to interpret it."

This prompted Sam to bring out her own list, the connections to the mysterious initials, which she'd garnered from the library.

"I might as well be keeping an eye out for anything that matches these, too," he said, pocketing the sheets of paper when their order arrived. "I spoke with Aiden and he may be calling later, once he gets back from Amarillo."

"That's quite a drive, both directions in one day."

Beau sampled the mashed potatoes on top of his portion. "Yeah, I thought so. But he's young and ambitious. Or maybe he'll be drop-dead tired and not call until tomorrow."

He glanced up, recognizing someone. "We've got company," Beau whispered, a hint of amusement in his voice as Samantha turned to see Melissa Fields approaching them.

"Beau, Samantha, how's it going in the detective game?" Melissa's shoulder-length hair swayed as she approached their table. It didn't appear anyone in the room had overheard her question.

Samantha smiled. "We're just digging, at this point."

"Join us?" Beau interjected, pushing aside his iced tea glass to make room for her at the table.

"I've had lunch, but I'll sit for a few minutes." Melissa's expression turned somber as she took an empty chair. "Mark's death hit us all hard, and Cecelia … well, she deserves answers."

"Cece tells me empathy is your superpower," Sam said, setting down her sandwich.

Even in her off-duty attire, the nurse's nurturing aura was palpable, a testament to her years of comforting those in need.

"Something like that," Melissa admitted, her eyes showing the depth of how she cared for others. "Look, something's been nagging at me, and I finally figured out what it was this morning."

They both directed quizzical looks toward her.

"I'd forgotten I still had this. The night I treated Mark's injuries from that beating, this fell on the floor in the ER. I stuck it in the pocket of a jacket I wear sometimes at work." She reached into a side pouch of her purse and pulled out something no larger than a quarter. Setting it on the table in front of Sam, she said, "I have no idea what it is. Well, I mean, I recognize a name on it, but I can't even guess why Mark would have had it."

# Chapter 15

Sam stared at what appeared to be a small metal medallion partially wrapped in paper.

"What is it?" Beau carefully unwrapped the paper from the object, holding them in each hand.

Melissa took a breath. "The paper has the name Cormorant Industries on it. It looks like maybe the header from an invoice or something, ripped from a larger sheet."

"And that tells us ... what?"

"Cormorant was a business here in town that made packaging materials. Don't ask me specifically what kind of packaging—I really don't know. I do know that there seemed to be quite a number of workplace injuries out there. In my student nursing days, I did rotations at a couple of clinics and the hospital, and we got a lot of their employees. Everything from cuts and gashes to missing fingers."

"Yowch."

"You said Cormorant *was* a business here?"

"Right. They shut down quite a while back. I'd guess fifteen years or more. Their warehouse sits out on the highway, maybe two miles toward Enid."

"It's still there?"

"Abandoned all this time."

"So, we have to wonder … how and when did Mark get this scrap?"

"And what about the medallion?" Sam turned the piece over in her fingers. "It has a loop at the top. Maybe it's a key fob decoration or something like that."

"That happens to be a little thing I do recognize," Melissa said with a smile. "One of the Cormorant employees I treated for a bonk on the head told me the company had awarded him the employee of the month medal, and he showed me one just like this."

Beau was chuckling. "Bonk on the head—is that a medical term?"

Their nurse friend blushed a little, wagging her head back and forth. "A mild concussion. It's what my grandma always called it when I pulled some stupid little stunt as a kid."

Sam was frowning over the medallion. "It's pretty crusty and corroded, but there is some kind of lettering. Maybe if we cleaned it up a bit."

"Mainly, you can recognize it by the company logo in the center. The bird. See?"

"That's a water bird," Beau mentioned. "Kind of an odd choice for a company in Oklahoma."

Melissa shrugged. "They're around. We have a lot of lakes and reservoirs." She patted the table top. "Anyway, I leave you to unravel the mystery. I gotta go."

As she walked away, Sam rewrapped the medallion in the paper scrap and tucked them into her own pocket. "Looks like I have something to puzzle over while you're delving into that journal."

They finished their lunch and walked out to their vehicles. The sun was bright, the November day warm and pleasant.

"Back to Cece's house?" Beau suggested.

"I'm ready. I'm itching to figure out what this latest clue means." She unlocked the SUV and climbed in, following Beau for the short trip.

She pulled the borrowed vehicle into its slot in the garage, while Beau left his outside. He walked through the doorway, motioning for Sam to pause a minute. As soon as he started searching the wheel wells and undercarriage, she knew what he was after. It only took a couple minutes for him to find it—a tracking device exactly like the one he'd removed from his truck.

Her eyes widened, but he put a finger to his lips. He dropped the small tracker into a trash can in the garage, replaced the lid on top, and they walked into the house.

Sam set her purse on the kitchen counter and turned to him. "Beau, do you think Sterling placed these on all employee vehicles?"

He shook his head. "I have no idea. Maybe only those who ask too many questions."

"Can you check the other cars—Cece's and the Corvette?"

"Good idea." He headed back out but returned in a few minutes. "The 'Vette had one, hers doesn't. At least, whoever was spying will now have no way to know when the vehicles leave the garage."

Sam thought back over the places she'd driven today, but decided none of it would look unusual.

Cecelia walked into the kitchen, setting a notebook on the counter and crossing to the coffee maker. "I need a pick-me-up. Did you guys get lunch?"

"Don't worry about us. Beau and I each have a project to research." Sam held up the paper-wrapped medallion, but Cece was already focused on her own project, the budget for the arts council's upcoming event.

While their hostess settled down to her own notes, Sam moved to the kitchen sink and used soap to scrub away the crusted dirt on the little medal. Under a bright light she was able to read the company name. On the back 'Employee of the Month' was prominent in embossed letters, but nothing personalized, nothing to identify who had received this particular award. She turned her attention to the scrap of paper it had been wrapped in.

It was in decent shape, faintly yellowed, but the paper was intact and had not seen exposure to the elements. If Cormorant Industries had gone out of business fifteen years ago, it seemed unlikely that Mark would just happen to come across these items lying on the ground.

She thought of what Melissa had told them about the abandoned facility. What if there were business records and papers still on the premises? If she and Beau were able to get inside, maybe they could figure out what track Mark had been on. She walked down the hall to the study to suggest the idea to Beau.

He was seated at the desk, bent over the open pages of the journal, muttering. "Obviously, Mark kept this record for his own knowledge, not really expecting anyone else to come along who would need to know what it says."

"I suppose that makes sense, in a way. He was probably gathering data—something to do with the accounting practices at the company—and most likely he intended to put it into a report of some kind, once he had it all figured out."

Beau stuck a sheet of paper into the page and closed the book. "So, what's up?"

She repeated her thoughts about the old records possibly still being on site at the abandoned Cormorant building, suggesting they could drive out and take a look.

"The name Cormorant is bugging me," he said. "Ever since we first heard it from Melissa, something about that name is familiar in some way. I just can't remember how or why."

"Maybe that's all the more reason to go out there and have a look around."

"I'm feeling skeptical about finding old records. If the company didn't take all their stuff when they left, surely vandals have had their way with the old building."

"Mark found these two things, and they must have meant something to his investigation of Sterling. I have to think they're connected somehow."

He reached out and took her hand. "You're right. Let's do it. Can't hurt to go and poke around, I suppose, and maybe something about the place will jog my memory."

Then his phone rang.

"It's Aiden," Beau said, picking it up and putting the call on speaker. "Hey man, you back in Creston already?"

"Not even close. I'll probably not hit town until close to midnight, but I wanted to let you know I got some interesting info on one of the families that disappeared.

Maybe we can meet for breakfast tomorrow and I can fill you in?"

"Sam and I had planned on going out to the abandoned Cormorant Industries building in the morning. Maybe we can meet later in the day? Or you might want to join us. I have a feeling it's either going to go pretty quickly or it'll take several hours."

"I know the place. I'll meet you out there in the morning. Two birds at once. What time?"

"You're the one who'll be up late tonight."

"Right. Let's make it seven in the morning. Bring flashlights. I'm sure the power has been cut off long ago."

The call ended and Sam gave Beau a wistful look. "Oh, to have the energy of the young."

# Chapter 16

The sun rose orange in the sky as Beau's truck rumbled to a stop outside the hulking remains of the factory, an enormous metal building with shipping bays at one end and a walk-through door near the other. Samantha hopped out, her sneakers crunching on the gravel, and she couldn't help but shiver as she took in the high, broken windows that stared like hollow eyes. The outside of the metal building had been heavily tagged with graffiti.

"Creepy," she muttered, pulling her jacket tighter around her.

"Kinda has its own charm, doesn't it?" Beau replied, flashing that lopsided grin that never failed to warm her. "But I'm glad I found and removed that tracker from my truck. I already feel like someone's several jumps ahead of us, since they probably tracked Mark out here at some point."

They were gathering their gear from the back seat of the truck when Aiden drove up. The investigator looked chipper enough, for someone who couldn't have gotten more than six hours of sleep. Sam tucked her backpack, with the carved box inside, under the seat. She hoped holding it on her lap on the way here had sent enough of its magical energy into her that she'd be able to see beyond the surface dirt of this place.

Aiden greeted them, saying he'd brought a heavy-duty flashlight and his camera. Beau gave more detail about why they were here—the fact that Mark Mitchell had two items from this business in his possession when he was beaten, weeks before his death—as he pulled out flashlights for himself and Sam. "We've got a lot of ground to cover," he said, staring up at the high garage doors.

They crunched over the weeds in the gravel lot, approaching the walk-in door. It was locked.

"Good thing I used to break into houses for a living," Sam said, reaching into the deep pocket of her jacket for her lock-picking tools.

Aiden gave Beau a look out of the corner of his eye but didn't say anything.

Within a minute, Sam was twisting the dirt-caked doorknob, letting them in. To their right was a cavernous space filled with complicated looking machinery. She turned to the men with a shrug.

"My guess, these are something that makes corrugated cardboard and then turns big sheets of it into boxes," Beau said. "Melissa said the business manufactured packaging supplies, and the logo on what was left of their sign shows a cardboard box."

"Logical enough," Aiden said, nodding. He shone

his flashlight around the space, verifying that the heavy machinery was about the only thing left. At the far righthand end of the space were the big rollup doors they'd seen from outside, most likely where trucks backed up to transport the finished products away.

They turned to their left, following the beam of Aiden's light. Two glassed-in offices stretched the width of the building. One still had a small sign above the door: Shop Foreman. Glancing into it, they noticed the only remaining items appeared to be a heavy metal desk and a file cabinet with drawers pulled halfway open.

Sam stepped inside and aimed her light toward the drawers. "Empty," she called out. The desk was more of a large worktable, with no drawers of its own. She rejoined the men.

A flight of metal stairs led up to a second floor above the offices. Beside the stairs, a metal door stood open, revealing a set of stairs leading down to another level.

"Let's split up." Beau suggested. "Aiden, basement's all yours. Sam, why don't you and I go upstairs and see if that's office space or storage?"

"Got it, boss. Give a shout if you see any ghostly factory workers," Aiden quipped, winking at Sam, who rolled her eyes but couldn't suppress a smile.

Beau walked ahead, testing each of the rusty stair treads as he put his weight on it. The thing seemed solid enough, and Sam followed. The door at the top of the stairs was securely locked, and Sam put her skills to work once more. When the metal door creaked open, it revealed the administrative area for the business.

"Holy cow," Sam whispered when they looked into the first office, which appeared to be an open-plan area for a half-dozen office staff.

Six desks sat in neat rows, chairs behind them, file cabinets flanking one entire wall. A computer terminal sat on each one, huge by today's standards, with chunky monitors and wires running everywhere.

"I wonder if these still work," Beau said, keeping his voice low, as every sound echoed throughout the place.

Sam flipped a wall switch beside the door. "No electricity. Aiden was right about that."

"So, there's no way to test the computers." Beau ran a finger over one of the monitors. "Plus, they're about an inch thick with dust."

"And cobwebs. Ugh."

"Should we take one with us? See if we can plug it in and get any information from it?" he asked.

Sam's eyes took in the stacks of file folders and paper on top of the file cabinets. "Even though they had computers, it appears they printed everything and then filed it. This was far from being a paperless operation."

"So …"

"So, whatever Mark found that relates to this business probably exists in print. Somewhere in this mess. We can't spend days and days at this, but look around. See if there's any reference to Sterling Enterprises, Sterling Microchips, or anyone we know of. Maybe Mark's name shows up, or maybe one of those people who mysteriously disappeared." Even as she said it, she realized what a stretch that would be.

Beau started at one end of the bank of file cabinets and she took the other.

Sam's fingers sifted through the detritus of forgotten paperwork, her eyes scanning for anomalies among the decay. Piles of yellowed documents and faded receipts teetered precariously on the brink of collapse around her. She was seeking a needle in a haystack—except the needle was a clue, and the haystack was the remnants of a once-thriving factory's paper trail. "Come on, Sam, where are you?" she muttered to herself, her brow furrowing in concentration.

And then, something caught her eye—a tattered corner peeking out from beneath a pile of old payroll sheets. Samantha pulled it free, revealing an aged newspaper sheet. As she scanned the headlines on the page, she caught the word Taos. Her pulse quickened. This was no coincidence.

"Beau … can you come over here?"

By the light of her flashlight, she skimmed the article, which covered a fatal vehicle accident in Taos County, New Mexico. Over her shoulder, Beau read along with her.

"You're quoted in here, hon," she said, a strange feeling settling in her belly. "Sheriff Beau Cardwell claims the accident is under investigation and results will be shared once his office has all the evidence."

"What newspaper *is* this?" He reached for the page and found the header. "The *Creston Gazette*. Why would they cover—"

"Beau! Samantha!" Aiden's voice boomed up the stairwell. "You're not going to believe this!"

At the sound of their names, Beau and Sam pivoted and rushed to the stairs. "Everything okay down there?" Beau shouted.

"Fine, but you need to see something. Now." They converged at the foot of the basement stairs, where Aiden stood aiming his light toward a huge safe.

"It's locked, of course. Sam? Any magic you can do on this one?"

His tone was joking, but she walked over to it and

placed her palms flat against the surface, on either side of the keypad. Closing her eyes she let images come to her as the heat from her hands warmed the cold steel. Behind her eyelids she saw numbers. 6-1-8-4-0-9. She asked for more light on the surface and pressed each digit, praying that the battery inside the device hadn't died long ago. When she reached for the handle, it turned easily and the door swung open.

Aiden appeared mildly freaked out. "Don't ask," Beau said. "It's just a talent of hers."

They all stared at the contents of the safe.

Ledgers, files, and bundles of cash were scattered among the three shelves inside. At the bottom of a pile of ledgers sat an old laptop computer.

She lifted one leatherbound book, squinting at an aged spine. "Project Phoenix" read the label in embossed letters that caught the scant light.

"Interesting," she mumbled to herself, flipping it open. Inside, diagrams and technical jargon painted a complex picture, but one image stood out—a microchip etched with a symbol of some kind. "This looks like important stuff, Beau. Why would they have closed the business and left this here?"

"Set the book back, Sam. We need to take a picture documenting what's here. We'll need time to decipher all this, so we're taking it. But I don't want there to be accusations that we've stolen anything," Beau said.

She stepped back and took several shots with her camera phone. The shelves with their bundles of cash, the file folders, all the breadcrumbs that would lead to the answers. She gathered the papers, evidence of something, she felt sure. Just not sure exactly what.

Aiden ran up the stairs and called down. "Somebody knows we're here."

Beau went on instant alert. "Who?"

"Not sure. But I heard a noise and saw a car cruise through the lot and out the other end."

"Maybe the old place has a security guard," Sam said. "Could explain why the whole site hasn't been ransacked."

"Not to put too fine a point on it, but we need to do our own bit of ransacking and get out of here." Beau scanned the space for a cardboard box, finding none. Ironic.

"Get what we can carry in our arms," Aiden suggested, "and let's stick it all in the trunk of my car and get going. We can go to my office and take our time with it."

"Close and lock the safe, Sam." Beau had his arms full, including the laptop and a lot of the file folders.

They made their way awkwardly up the stairs to the ground level, where Aiden peered out one of the broken windows. "Looks clear."

Sam took the time to lock the exterior door and then rushed to join the men and stash the Phoenix Project book with the rest of it. Her heart was pounding as Beau started his truck and they drove out, taking a leisurely pace, as if they'd merely been sightseeing.

No other vehicles appeared to be on the property, but as they turned east, toward Enid, she spotted one of Rollie Benson's Creston PD patrol cars to the west. Her stomach lurched.

# Chapter 17

"The place is lowkey, but I do have good security," Aiden said, as they furtively carried their haul from the warehouse into his office and he set the alarm system.

"First of all, the cash goes into my office safe until we figure out who it rightfully belongs to." He picked up the bundles, about two thousand dollars in all, and stashed them. "Now, what's next? Did you guys have breakfast before we met? I'm starving."

"Toast," Sam said, "and I'm getting hungry too. I guess breaking and entering burns a lot of calories."

"We can make it a working lunch, breakfast, whatever … if we get some kind of takeout," Beau said. "I'll even pick it up."

There was a brief discussion on the merits of pizza, Chinese, or Thai. Aiden phoned the order to his favorite pizza place, and Beau was on the way.

"I'm glad he removed the tracker from his truck," Sam said, watching from the front window.

"What? I don't think I knew about this." Aiden's face registered shock.

"Oh yeah, the second day we were here and the only place we went was out to Sterling Enterprises. We found the same devices on Mark's personal vehicle."

"So there really was something to his suspicions about his employer."

"I doubt they can give any reasonable explanation for the trackers. It's made me wonder if that's an accessory every employee gets," Sam said with a wry grin. "Or maybe it's only for those who ask too many questions."

"Speaking of which, the story I heard from that former Sterling employee in Amarillo will raise your hackles."

"Did they also get tracking devices?"

"Didn't mention it, but now that I know this, it makes a lot of sense. Shall I tell the whole story now, or do we wait for Beau?"

"Let's wait for Beau. Meanwhile, we could see about organizing what we brought back from the box factory." Sam's fingers skimmed over the file folders, but her real interest was in the laptop, which she carried to one end of their long worktable. "Aiden, I'm sure you are far better at this kind of thing than either Beau or I. Do you think you can find anything on it?"

He raised the lid and touched the power button but, of course, nothing happened. "Let's see if I can come up with a cord for it." He disappeared through a doorway that revealed a storage room.

Sam read through the labels on the file folders, not terribly surprised when she came to a file with Project

Phoenix emblazoned across the front. She set it next to the leatherbound book with the same title. That would bear closer scrutiny.

By the time Aiden came back with several power cords in hand, she'd also come across a file on Sterling Microchips.

"Phoenix … rising from the ashes," Aiden mused, noticing the items she'd set aside. "Okay, let's plug this baby in and see what happens." One of the cords had the correct size connector, so he inserted it and plugged it into the wall.

"Come on, come on," he muttered, willing the screen to light up.

Nothing.

"Let's give it a while to recharge the battery," he suggested. "There could still be hope. If that doesn't work, I know a guy."

They sorted folders until the sound of Beau's truck got their attention. Aiden let him in and reset the alarm. "No one trailing you?" He wasn't joking.

Beau set the large supreme on the table, away from the paperwork, and they washed their hands and took seats.

"Aiden thinks the family who fled for Texas may have been tracked, as well," Sam said, choosing a slice and biting into the heavenly combination of pepperoni, veggies, and cheese.

"What's their story?" Beau's attention didn't waver.

"Jamie and Chelsea Braddock. They're in their thirties, with two young kids. Chelsea worked at Sterling, same department as Mark. Apparently the two talked sometimes and she told Mark about some irregularities she'd noticed with shipments. An order would be for, say, twelve thousand chips but the packing slip might say ten thousand. It's just one digit, could be a typo. But she saw it fairly often. Whenever she brought it to the attention of the department supervisor, they snatched the invoice away from her and said they'd take care of it."

"Where were this lady and Mark when they talked? Was it on company property?" Beau asked.

"Sometimes at one of their desks, sometimes in the lunch room."

Beau nodded.

"Then one day Chelsea finds a note in her desk drawer: How much do you love your kids? They attend Happy Place Day School, don't they?"

"Ohmygosh," Sam said. "My blood would run cold if I saw that."

"Hers did. They pulled the kids from school for a few days, claiming they'd caught colds, and Chelsea stayed home with them."

"But that can't go on forever, right?"

"Sterling pays their people very well," Aiden said. "Chelsea's salary was a huge portion of their income. She went back to work and Jamie stayed home with the kids for a few days. But then Chelsea finds another note, this one inside her purse, which had been locked in her desk drawer."

"What did that one say?" Sam set her pizza slice on her paper plate.

"It was nothing but a list of names. Chelsea was only familiar with two of them, but she knew what it meant. They were among the ones who had disappeared. That night they packed their car and headed for her parents home in Tulsa."

"But they didn't stay in Tulsa …"

"Because that's when the calls started. Not on Chelsea's company phone—she'd left that one behind. This was on her parents' landline."

"Damn." Beau's face had grown pale.

"The Braddocks figured their car had been recognized, maybe their license plate was on some kind of watch list by the police. They traded the car and got another, and moved their little brood to Amarillo. They were all set to figure out how to change their names, go completely off the grid, but then the calls stopped. She and her mother got prepaid phones and stayed in touch, and Mom says no more calls came."

"I bet they were kind of freaked out that you found them."

"To say the least. It was only the mention of Mark Mitchell's name that convinced them I was on their side. And they've already said they will not return to Oklahoma in person to testify against anyone at Sterling. They are well and truly terrified."

"We have to solve this," Sam said. "Imagine all those families who felt scared enough to leave."

"Not to mention the ones we suspect were kidnapped and held somewhere in order to intimidate them into quitting and not talking about it." Beau's face was grim.

"It's become even more serious than that, Sam. Mark may have received similar threats and thought he could ignore them. For that, he was beaten once and then killed. Whatever he and certain coworkers found, it's become deadly."

Beau wiped his mouth with a napkin and turned down another slice of pizza. "Back to what we discovered today at the warehouse. We went there because of the medallion Mark had at the time he was beaten up. What proof do we have there's any connection between the two places—Sterling and Cormorant?"

"Well, I'll show you," Sam said, proudly pulling some of the folders closer. "Look what we found in Cormorant's safe—two files on Sterling Microchips."

Finally, Beau smiled.

After they'd finished their lunch and cleared the table, Aiden tried the laptop again. This time, his persistence paid off. A faint glow emerged and the screen lit up, revealing a terribly outdated operating system. "Bingo."

Samantha peered over his shoulder, eyes narrowing. "Can you really get anything off that thing?"

"Watch me. I actually used this system back in my military days." Aiden's confidence was infectious. He worked quickly with a few keystrokes, getting into the hard drive files behind the upfront operating system. Strings of letters and numbers danced across the screen like digital confetti. Encrypted messages appeared, a jumble of letters and numbers.

"Now we need an experienced code-breaker," Sam mumbled.

Aiden looked up. "As I said, I know a guy. I'll copy a short passage of this and see if he can make sense of it. As long as it seems safe, we'll proceed. If it looks like dangerous stuff, we'll turn it all over to the authorities." He saw Beau's expression. "Not the locals."

"And by extension, I'd still like to know what the connection is between Creston and Taos."

"Other than yourself?" Aiden took in Beau's startled expression. "You grew up here, and you live there now. It's a connection."

"Everything's connected in some way. We just have to figure it out," Beau added "That factory, is not just some abandoned relic. It was a hub of some kind."

"Creston and Taos, Sterling and Cormorant," Samantha said, her voice echoing Beau's earlier discovery, "they're not just random dots on a map. But I have no idea what's behind all this."

Beau shook it off. "It's something other than that. Let me make a call or two."

While Sam turned back toward the file folders strewn across the table, Beau pulled out his phone and tapped a familiar number.

"Hey, it's Beau Cardwell. I need to talk to Evan. Yeah, it's urgent." He paced a narrow path between the worktable and the window.

"Hey, Evan," Beau continued, leaning against Aiden's filing cabinet, "we've stumbled onto something big in Oklahoma. It ties a certain Cormorant Industries, and perhaps Sterling Microchips, back to Taos." His eyebrows drew together as he listened to the voice on the other end of the line. Samantha could tell from the creases in his forehead that the current sheriff was talking as he searched records.

"Interesting," she muttered to herself, leaning closer to her notebook when she came to a page of words that seemed to be a code, although different from the computer code Aiden had found on the laptop.

"Call me back when you find more." Beau finished his call and turned to Samantha, his expression intense. "Evan's going to dig around."

"Good," Samantha said, tapping her pencil against

her chin. "Because I think I'm onto something with these messages." Her eyes sparkled with the thrill of the chase, and she shared a look with Beau.

"Can you decode them, Sam?" Beau encouraged, his trust in her skills absolute. "Whatever you find, it could break this wide open."

The power from the box was wearing off and she didn't feel confident, but she turned back to her notes. At home she and Kelly had inherited a book written in cryptic messages, a tome they referred to as their book of runes, which neither of them could read unless they'd handled the wooden boxes. As with that book, on the pages before her now, the numbers and letters seemed to dance before her eyes, and then they formed words.

# Chapter 18

The Phoenix is dying," she read from the page. "Okay, guys, what does that even mean?"

She received shrugs from both men. Her head was beginning to pound and Beau saw the signs that she was getting weary from the effort.

"Let's take a break from all this," he suggested. "Maybe we aren't seeing things clearly because we're all on information overload."

Aiden nodded, although his eyes went back to the screen of the laptop on the table. "I'll let you know if my buddy says that short passage of code means anything. You want to take all these files with you?"

Beau spoke up. "We could. Cece has a secure place for them."

Sam decided she might take the leatherbound book,

the Phoenix Project material. "Once I shed this headache maybe I can make more sense of it."

They packed the files into a manageable stack in a storage box, which Beau carried out to the truck. When they arrived at Cecelia's house, she wasn't there.

"Oh well," Beau said, setting the heavy box on the floor in Mark's study. "We can have her open the safe for us later."

Sam went upstairs to their room and settled in for a few minutes of deep-breathing, trying to quiet her mind after the long morning of discoveries. Her headache abated and she picked up her phone to check in with Kelly.

"Hey, Mom. How's Oklahoma?"

"Confusing. How are things at home?"

"Same. I still don't know what's going on with Riki, why she's hit this *mood* she can't shake. She sent me home early today, which was fine. I've got plenty to do around the house here."

"Maybe she's pregnant. They've been wanting it to happen."

"Nah, I don't think it's that. She'd be floating on cloud nine." Something metallic crashed in the background. "Sorry. Dropped a skillet. I'm trying a new chicken dish tonight."

"Change of subject. Kel, have you ever heard of a business called Cormorant Industries?"

"Local?"

"No, they're located here, just outside Creston, but we found something that ties to Taos. Just thought you might have heard someone, maybe a customer at Puppy Chic, mention the name. Anyway, Beau's got Evan checking on it."

"Sorry, I don't think I'm much help on this one."

"Well, if you hear anything …"

"Have you talked to Jen? She's always chatting up the bakery customers and probably knows a whole lot more people in this town than I do."

"Good idea. I'd planned to give her a call anyway, so I'll do that. Meanwhile, how are Ana and Scott?"

Kelly went into a tale about how her husband got himself into a pickle when he took their five-year-old to one of the town's historic homes. It seemed little Ana knew more about the famous artist who lived there and their body of work than the docent did, and things got a little sticky as other patrons began paying more attention to the child.

"She's a smart kid," Sam said. "You do know we'll have to watch out for how much she picks up about those couple of artifacts you keep in the house."

"Oh, that's already happened. She caught me flipping through the book of runes one afternoon when I thought she was napping. She could read the symbols right off the page."

Which reminded Sam she had planned on going back through the notes she'd been working on earlier. They ended the call and she picked up her backpack and retrieved the box. Carrying it under one arm, she sank into a comfortable wingback chair in the corner while placing a call to her business at home.

"Sweet's Sweets, how may I assist you?" came Jen's friendly voice. When she realized who it was, she became even more bubbly "Sam! How is everything with you and Beau—how's his cousin doing?"

Sam assured her the visit was going well. She hadn't let on that they were working on a murder case, merely that this was a family visit to someone recently widowed. Then she posed the question about whether Jen had ever heard the name Cormorant Industries.

"Cormorant … like, boxes and crates?"

"Um, yes, exactly. What do you know about them?"

"Not a lot. Back when I worked at that gallery, the owner purchased specialized containers for artwork that needed to be shipped. I have no idea why that name came to me just now."

"Well, it was a good one. It was a company near here, but they are out of business now."

"Are you two working on some kind of a case?" Jen asked with a laugh.

"Yeah, I guess I have to admit it. We came across a scrap of something that ties Cormorant to Taos, and I'm trying to make sense of it."

"Well, aside from the gallery and maybe some other local customers, I can't think what it would be. In other news …" Jen said, waiting a beat, "… we'll be super busy when you get back. Nancy Whitson with the Chamber of Commerce is organizing a big event and they want our pumpkin pies. Plus, the orders for Thanksgiving are rolling in and your cranberry-apple pie tops the list."

The reminder of the holiday made Sam wish she was home, waiting for the first significant snowfall and preparing for the festivities. But she set that longing aside. They had a job to do here. She signed off, telling Jen to say hello to the rest of the crew and to call if they needed anything.

Rubbing her hands together and setting the carved box back in the drawer, she again picked up the file and book labeled Project Phoenix. This time when she opened the cover, the words came through crystal clear. There was a lot of technical-speak about computer chips, which she didn't come close to understanding. Skimming through that, she spotted two crucial names and a passage that seemed to mean something:

Meeting—Jay Cormorant and Olivia Sterling. Phoenix is on hold, probably permanently.

Olivia Sterling had met with the Cormorant CEO? The date on the meeting notes was a year or more before the packaging company had shut down, if Melissa's estimate was correct. And it was slightly before the new Sterling Microchips plant opened here in Creston.

What was the significance of that?

She picked up the papers and went downstairs in search of Beau, locating him in the kitchen where he was seated at the island counter with a beer stein in hand. Cecelia stood in front of the open refrigerator door.

"Hey, Sam, I'm trying to decide what's for dinner. The bane of every woman's existence, right?"

"I ate enough pizza for lunch that you don't need to worry about me. Open a can of soup, if you want to." Sam realized how that sounded. "Sorry, I didn't mean to be rude. But really, anything at all will be fine. Don't do anything big or fancy."

Cece closed the fridge door and poured herself a glass of wine. "This will do for starters, then we'll play it by ear."

Beau reached out and ran his arm around Sam's waist. "You seem like you came in here with some news. Find something exciting?"

"There's a connection between Cormorant Industries and Olivia Sterling." She read from the coded page and told them her theory about the timeline. "It looks to me like the CEO, Jay Cormorant, was trying to work some kind of deal with Sterling but it fell through."

"Reading a little mythology into it," Cecelia said, "maybe Cormorant's business was dying and he hoped this so-called Project Phoenix would help to raise it from the ashes."

Beau pondered her words. "Could be valid. The way they simply shut down their plant here, not clearing out equipment or paperwork, was curious. If they were planning to relocate, they would have moved everything. If it was a liquidation, I'd think they would have sold everything, including the building."

"That makes a lot of sense," Sam said, laying the open book on the counter while she walked over to the cupboard in search of a glass. Filling it from the fridge's water dispenser, she turned back to Beau. "We need to interview Olivia Sterling."

"You haven't talked to her yet?" Cece asked.

"We never got beyond Jason Blackwood when we went out there. And he wasn't exactly welcoming."

"Nor was he sharing any information with us."

"In fairness, he didn't know us from Adam and no one in his position would be willing to reveal company secrets," Beau said, emptying his mug.

"Yes, but. We weren't out there asking for company secrets. We wanted to know more about what happened to Mark. A little cooperation, by showing us the security footage or something … that would have been helpful."

"Sam, it's too late for that. He's not going to give up those things, even if they do exist."

"So, we'll see if we can go over his head. And once you flash those fabulous eyes at Olivia Sterling, she'll melt and she'll be willing to give us whatever we need."

"Dreamer." But he laughed.

Sam turned to Cece. "Your cousin always had a way with interviews and usually got exactly the information he needed. Especially with the ladies."

"Dreaming and delusional," he teased.

She flashed him a saucy smile and again turned to his cousin. "Do you have any kind of an 'in' with Olivia Sterling? Some way to get us an interview?"

Cece shrugged. "We're not exactly chums. But she, like everyone else at the time Mark died, said if there was ever anything she could do for me …"

"Use it. Say your cousin is in town and—I don't know—that we'd like to meet the wonderful employer who gave Mark his job." Sam waved her arms in a flourish.

"Maybe it would be better to drop by, pretend it's a social call, introduce y'all to her, and then let Beau work that sheriff-magic of his."

"You ladies are teasing me, but okay. Let's try that."

# Chapter 19

After being announced by the polite woman at the reception desk, they were met at the top of the stairs by the CEO herself. Cool and surface-polite, Olivia Sterling held out a hand to Cecelia. With her blonde hair pulled back into a precise bun, her navy business suit and four-inch heels, she set herself apart from most of the women in Creston. Sam guessed her to be thirty-five or so, a self-made woman.

"Cecelia, how are you these days?" The well-modulated voice carried exactly the proper tone of concern, certainly not any more.

"I'm coping." She introduced Beau and Sam as cousins from New Mexico. "Do you have a few minutes? I really do have something I'd like to talk about."

Sam had to admire the small catch that came into

Cece's voice at this last part. There was no way Olivia could gracefully refuse. She led the way to her office, a large suite at the end of the hall, with tall windows facing the leafy trees that lined the creek, as bucolic a scene as one would find in that part of the country. Her space made the statement that Jason Blackwell's office put him definitely second in the pecking order around here.

Cecelia took one of the chairs in the informal grouping beside a glassed-in fireplace. "You know, Olivia, that I never accepted Rollie Benson's decision to close Mark's case."

"I know. I know ..." Olivia stopped just short of calling her sweetie, as if she were ninety years old. "And I felt so horrible that our security footage was lacking in that part of the garage."

"As a newcomer to Oklahoma, you may not realize how deep Rollie's ties to this town are, and how he fancies himself as kind of our little overlord."

Olivia allowed a small wrinkle to crease her forehead, but she didn't say anything.

"Anyway," Cecelia took a deep breath, "that's why I invited Beau here. He's had a long career in law enforcement—sheriff of Taos County—and I hoped he might spot something missing from the local investigation."

Olivia shifted in her chair, recrossing her legs. "And have you? Found something Rollie didn't catch?" She looked toward Beau and Sam.

He took the ball. "Unfortunately, Chief Benson has not been forthcoming in sharing any of the files, so we've been on our own with this."

Sam watched the exchange, looking for nuances, reading Olivia's aura, which seemed a little murkier as the conversation went on. She reminded herself that

Mark's investigation had been focused on some type of irregularities in the accounting department of this corporation; they had to expect that Olivia would admit nothing.

Beau changed tracks. "Tell me about the security measures here on the grounds and in the parking garage."

Olivia straightened her spine. "Top notch. As you've seen, upon arrival each visitor is greeted at the guard gate and logged in. At the front desk everyone is asked to state their business. Ninety percent of visitors already have an appointment and their name will be checked against a list the guards have."

"And for your employees?"

"Employee stickers on their vehicles, ID badges worn on lanyards while in the building. The ID badge allows access only to those areas necessary to their jobs. For instance, administrative personnel do not have access to the production plant floor. That's mainly a cleanliness concern, as the manufacture of chips requires a completely dust-free environment. Workers in the plant go through a vacuum chamber that removes loose particles and they wear special suits, booties, hair covers, and gloves."

"Right. That makes sense." Beau rubbed his chin. "And before they enter the building? Out in the employee parking garage?"

"Cameras record every vehicle coming and going, and until this incident, I thought virtually every square foot of the garage was covered on camera, in order to see who gets out of each vehicle, who approaches the elevators. Where, by the way, the employee must scan their badge before the elevator doors will open."

"Sounds very thorough."

"It is, and we pride ourselves on our safety record. In the ten years this plant has been open, we've had not one workplace injury that required medical attention."

"Until Mark," Cece interjected.

Olivia's mouth crimped in a sympathetic-seeming downturn. She nodded, blinking rapidly.

Beau took a breath and switched topics. "What do you know about Cormorant Industries?"

"What? Cormorant ... Well, that's a blast from the past," Olivia said with a puzzled little smile.

"Your company and Cormorant were in some sort of negotiation, sounded like a very big contract."

"Potentially. We never reached an agreement and it came to nothing."

"Tell us more." Sam leaned forward.

"There's not much to tell. Jay Cormorant headed a talented team who could come up with packaging and shipping solutions for nearly any product. We thought, being another local manufacturer, they might be good to work with, a partnership that would boost Creston's economy in positive ways. Jay himself was all business. Asian. Maybe that's their nature. I don't know. But when we did our due diligence on his company's finances, it appeared they would not be the right match for us."

"Because ..."

"Frankly, they were in trouble. Cormorant was hanging by a thread, financially, and we couldn't take the risk of being pulled down with them."

"So, they wanted more than to become Sterling's supplier, they wanted a partnership?"

"Exactly. A multi-million dollar buyout where we simply got innovative packaging for our products and they

got a huge infusion of cash. It wasn't to our advantage."
Olivia cleared her throat. "I don't see how any of this
relates to what happened to Mark Mitchell."

"You're right, it doesn't seem to connect. Just one of
those threads." Beau gave a tiny shake of his head. "Could
you give us access to the security video from the night
Mark died? Even if it doesn't seem to show anything, I'd
like to take a look."

Sam watched as a new emotion showed on Olivia's
face. Relief? It didn't seem logical.

"I will have to put you in touch with Jason Blackwood,
my second in command, for that. I know we have a whole
room devoted to the security of this building, and I know
where it's located. Running all of it, as they say, is not my
department." She scooted forward in her chair. "I'll see if
he's available."

They waited as she walked over to her desk and picked
up the phone, pressing two digits on the keypad. Sam and
Beau exchanged a look as Olivia confirmed that Jason was
available to show them what they wanted to know. She
ushered them out into the hall, where they spotted Jason
emerging from his office. The two executives exchanged
a warm smile, and Olivia told him to show them to the
security room before she closed herself back in her own
office.

Jason stiffened when he recognized them, but Sam
noticed he didn't say anything in front of Olivia to
acknowledge their previous visit. And some kind of weird
vibe passed between Jason and Cecelia as the corporate v.p.
led the way through a maze of hallways and key-carded his
way into an unmarked room.

A bank of video monitors filled one wall, and three

men sat at a desk, leaning back in high-backed leather chairs.

"Carson, these are visitors from New Mexico. Ms. Sterling has asked that you answer whatever questions Sheriff Cardwell has."

The eldest of the three men nodded and shook Beau's extended hand. "Sheriff, huh. I was in law enforcement myself, twenty-two years. Retired from county to come here about eight years ago." He lowered his voice. "Private sector pays better."

Beau nodded and smiled. A rapport was established, and that was his goal. As he went into his questions about the camera coverage and how long they kept the surveillance video, Sam stepped to the back of the small room.

Cecelia and Jason had hung back, and she now caught a few whispers between them. She tuned her ear in their direction. When she caught the words "I haven't said anything" from Cece, her reaction must have showed.

Jason nudged Cece's arm and announced he had a phone call to make. "I'll have someone escort your group out when you're finished here," he said.

Sam watched him exit, spine stiff, face unsmiling. What was that about? But this was not the place to bring it up.

# Chapter 20

If Beau noticed the stiffness between the two women during the ride back to Cecelia's house, he didn't show it. He led the conversation with a rehash of what they'd learned at Sterling. He seemed convinced of the limitations of the security cameras on the night of the murder, although a new camera had been installed to cover the blank area since then.

"I wasn't all that convinced with what Olivia said about Cormorant," he added. "Her basic story that the merger never happened because of Cormorant's weak financial position—that may be true. But we know, from the Cormorant records, that there was more to it. I'd like to see if I can locate this Jay Cormorant and get his side of the story."

He pulled into the driveway at Cecelia's house and

they all filed inside, Sam heading directly upstairs to their bedroom. He walked in a minute later.

"You seemed pretty quiet on the way back," he said, looking concerned.

"I overheard Jason and Cece whispering at the back of the room while you were talking to the security guy. One of the things she said to him was that she hadn't 'said anything'. I don't know, Beau. The whole exchange just sounded … intimate."

He froze. "You think the two of them were … up to something?"

"I have no idea. I just found it really strange that she hasn't said anything to us about knowing any of these Sterling folks on any level other than as Mark's employers. What did she say—the occasional office Christmas party? But what I overheard was a lot more cozy than that."

"Okay. Well, we have to know. Come on." He flung open the bedroom door and headed downstairs, his boots practically thundering in the marble foyer. "Cecelia! Living room. We need to talk."

She emerged from the kitchen, a little cowed. Beau paced the length of her living room, his hands balled into fists at his sides, as she edged toward the sofa. "What's going on?"

"What were you and Jason Blackwood whispering about back there, earlier? Something about you hadn't told us something?"

Sam admired the way he made it sound as though he were the one who overheard, but she felt a flush of embarrassment that she'd ratted on his cousin. Still, it was a fact and they needed to get to the bottom of it.

"Cece, what are you hiding?"

Her fingers twisted the hem of her tunic top, her gaze anchored to the floor. "I really never wanted this to come out." Her eyes were miserable when she looked back up. "Jason came on to me."

"Recently? Since Mark——?"

"No, this was right from the beginning. As soon as Mark took the job at Sterling and we were included in company social functions. Jason was subtle about it, flirting, teasing. But it was right under Mark's nose."

"Were you tempted?" Sam asked, as gently as she could.

"No! I loved Mark, and we were a team."

"But …"

"Okay, Jason is a good-looking man and he can be persuasive. There was one Christmas party and I'd had too much to drink. He pulled me into a side room and we were kissing, and I never meant it to go even that far." Her face crumpled. "I ducked out and rejoined the group, but from that moment I knew Jason had it in for us—for me and Mark."

"In what way?"

"Threats at work. Mark's job seemed to be on the line, a lot. Mistakes were blamed on him, accusations made openly rather than handled discreetly."

"And so Mark decided to dig deeper, find some dirt on Jason or the company in general …"

Cecelia shrugged. "I don't know if it became a tit-for-tat thing or if Mark already had his suspicions. He quit telling me things. Jason started putting even more pressure on me, hinting that if he and I were lovers, then Mark would have an easier time at work. Hinting that I should leave Mark for him. I was scared, Beau." Her eyes met his, wide and pleading. "Scared of what he might do next."

Samantha leaned against the doorframe, her arms crossed. She saw the storm behind Beau's eyes. But she also saw the sliver of pain there, the hurt that Cecelia had caused. She also knew all too well the reputation Jason held—ambitious, shrewd, and not above playing dirty. It made sense, too much sense, and that worried her.

"Jason is dangerous, but I had no idea he might go so far as to have Mark killed," Cecelia continued, her voice steadying with resolve. "And then when you came and started asking questions, I couldn't risk y'all getting hurt too."

"Do you think Jason was the one who actually did the stabbing?" Beau's tone was point-blank, almost cold.

Cece shook her head. "I honestly don't know. Today was the first time I've seen him since Mark's funeral." Her face crumpled in tears.

Beau exhaled slowly, his gaze never leaving Cecelia's face. Samantha could see him sifting through the layers, searching for truth among the fear and doubt.

Cecelia nodded, relief softening her features for a brief moment. "I do know that Jason has Chief Benson under his thumb. It's got to be the reason the police investigation went nowhere."

"Okay," he finally said, though the single word landed heavy in the room. "We'll figure this out."

But Sam felt lingering doubts. Could Cecelia really be entangled with Blackwood? Was she part of this twisted plot? She knew Beau had a good read on people, could sniff out a lie like a bloodhound. But Cecilia's plea seemed sincere, her eyes wide pools of earnestness.

"We'll work on this together," Beau finally said. "But I need the whole truth, Cecelia. No more secrets."

"Of course," Cecelia agreed quickly, almost too quickly. "Anything you need."

"Does anyone else know about this little … whatever it was? You've got to understand how it would look," he said, his voice low and even.

She shook her head. "We were alone, that time at the Christmas party. No one saw or overheard."

"Would Jason have told anyone?" Sam asked. "Certain men will brag, even about things that never happened."

Cece's face went white. "Oh, God, I hope not."

Sam stepped toward her husband, meeting his eyes. "She's scared, Beau. But not lying."

"I know. I know, but that man could have done a lot of damage. We all need to be alert, with everyone we talk to, looking for signs that Jason ordered Mark's death. If we hear anything, we need to get evidence." He turned toward his cousin. "And Cece, no more surprises."

# Chapter 21

I'm going to get some air," Beau said, the strain of the conversation still evident on his face. He grabbed his Stetson and walked out the front door, heading toward the center of town.

It had been an eventful morning, and he always had a hard time when someone in his trusted inner circle proved to be deceitful. Thoughts about Cece and Jason Blackwood filled his head, along with the visit with Olivia Sterling this morning. His lawman-radar told him there were a lot of secrets surrounding the woman and her successful company.

And it wouldn't surprise him a bit if Olivia and Jason were up to their necks in a conspiracy to downplay Mark's death. If they had already convinced the local cops that the murder was completely unrelated to company business, it was ninety percent of the battle. Who else was going to dig into it?

He was.

His stride picked up urgency. That pair definitely hadn't counted on Cecelia bringing in a cousin with a law enforcement background. And whether he was officially on duty or not, Beau Cardwell would pursue this in the same professional manner that he would with another case.

He'd reached a park, where a group of people were gathered around the bandstand, milling about, putting up decorations. He kept to the perimeter, not wanting to get into a distracting conversation.

By the time he'd circled the park and headed back into his cousin's neighborhood, he knew what he would say.

\* \* \*

Sam watched Beau walk away from the house, until he was out of sight around a corner. When she turned toward the room, Cecelia was sitting on one of the couches, her head in her hands.

"I've really made a mess of everything, haven't I? Y'all must not believe a word I've said now."

Sam crossed the room and sat in a chair across from her. "It would have been better to tell us more about Jason and his motives, right from the start. You have to understand Beau's thinking from a law enforcement viewpoint. A crucial fact omitted is pretty much the same as a lie, to him."

"I just didn't think—" Cece's shoulders slumped. "That's the problem. I just didn't think."

"Beau's mainly worried about what you might have inadvertently revealed to Jason, whether the man was quizzing you without your knowing it."

"I know. It's eating me up, thinking I might have said something that made them angry enough to kill Mark for what he was digging into. But, Sam, I swear I didn't *know* anything. Mark truly did keep company secrets to himself."

Maybe not completely to himself, Sam thought. What if he'd talked with someone else? Ethan at the library knew Mark had done some computer searches that he didn't want to work on at home. Aiden had found notes tying Mark to Cormorant Industries, and Lucy Evergreen realized Mark's notations had something to do with accounting, therefore, presumably, Mark's job. There were any number of people who could have said the wrong thing to the wrong person. She rubbed her temples. There were simply too many what-ifs.

"Sam, you look like you could use a cup of tea," Cece offered. "Or maybe a little lunch?"

"Tea sounds good."

The kettle had just whistled, and Sam was debating between an Indian Assam and an English teatime blend, when they heard the front door. Beau was back.

* * *

He paced the kitchen, somehow not yet depleted of energy even though the walk had been a long one.

"Cece, you good with digging up what you can on Blackwood?"

"A little nervous. But I'll do it. Whatever it takes."

"Will he believe it if you want to meet for a drink or something like that?"

Her eyes widened. "I don't know … I was flat-out in my refusal."

Sam stepped forward and gave Cece a level look. "That man still has hopes. I saw his body language today."

"And you told us he'd kept pressing you to get involved with him, even after the Christmas party." Beau took a long breath. "It'll have to be subtle. He'll be suspicious if you call him right away and say you've changed your mind."

"I couldn't!"

"But—if you were to accidentally run into him somewhere, sit next to him at the bar or something …"

She pursed her mouth thoughtfully. "That might work."

"Do you know where he hangs out after work? He's a single guy, and even though he probably has some luxury digs, most likely he doesn't go straight home alone. Did Mark ever mention a watering hole where company guys went, anything like that?"

"Depends on which set of guys," she said with a smile. "I think the factory workers went to this little honkytonk in Enid. Bigger town, more of that kind of thing. The executives … I'm not—wait. Olivia had a paper coaster on the table in her office; it came from The Briar Club."

"Is that a private club?" Sam asked.

"Oh, no. It's just got a fancy name. I've been there with Mark a time or two. It's got the kind of upscale exterior and bouncers wearing ties, so the appearance of it discourages the riff-raff."

"Would you be comfortable going in there alone? I have a feeling if Beau and I were with you it would dampen Mr. Blackwood's enthusiasm."

"Could y'all be right outside, in case things go …"

Beau nodded. He wanted information but wasn't willing to let his cousin take real risks with her safety.

"When?"

"Tonight? I'd guess he'll be leaving work in an hour or so." Cecelia took a deep breath, visibly working up her courage.

"You certain you're okay with this?" Sam asked.

"Like Beau said, Jason surely knows things. I don't know what information I can get, but I'll surely try."

"Put on your best actor's face and you'll do fine."

* * *

At five-thirty, they watched Cecelia walk into The Briar Club, wearing a lowcut blue dress and heels that begged for attention. Her bright yellow jacket had pockets, and she'd been instructed to place her phone in the one on whichever side Jason was sitting. When she spotted his approach, she would activate a phone call to Beau. It was the next best thing to wearing a wire, and the only thing they could come up with on short notice.

"Don't move around a lot, or the fabric of your jacket will cause distortion," Beau had instructed. "And don't let your drink out of your sight."

"Yes, Daddy," she'd teased. "For your information, it's not my first time to walk into a bar."

Sam felt on pins and needles, waiting out in the SUV, not knowing whether Jason was already here or if he would arrive at all.

Beau's phone rang and he picked it up.

"He's here," came Cece's whisper, then some rustling as she slid the phone into her pocket, walked across the room, and took a seat.

"I hope she remembered to mute our voices," Sam mouthed.

Beau shrugged. They couldn't be sure about that.

A couple minutes passed and they faintly heard Cece order a bourbon. Then a male voice, closer. "Well, well, fancy seeing you here."

"Jason? Oh my gosh. I somehow imagined that you live 24/7 at the office."

"Nope, nope." A pause. "So, where's your company?"

"My cousin and his wife? Well, you know. A person can take just so much family before they need a break."

Sam looked at Beau. Was she serious?

Cecelia laughed. "But these aren't among that bunch. We're doin' great. They had to run into the city to, uh, spend an evening with some other friends. And I decided it was high time I got out of the house."

"Well, here's to getting out of the house." Glasses clinked. "I've thought a lot about you, Cecelia. These last few months must have been so hard."

A lengthy silence, in which Beau imagined a nod, perhaps a pat on the arm.

"You know … I'd be there for you, whatever you need." His tone seemed like that of a caring friend. Until he spoke again. "*Whatever* you need."

This time Beau imagined the pause being because Cece wanted to kick the guy where it hurt.

She cleared her throat before speaking. "Jason, I do appreciate your concern. I just—" a little hitch in her voice "—I just need to know what happened to Mark before I can move on. The police gave me so little to go on, and it's … well, it's eatin' away at me. If somebody could just set my mind at ease, you know."

Sensing that he wasn't about to have a good time tonight, Jason's tone changed. "I wish I knew."

"You haven't heard things—rumors around the office?"

Silence. Maybe he was shaking his head. Beau wished Cece would prompt him.

"Come on, Jason, nothing?"

Ice rattled in a glass, and low-level sounds muffled the voices until his came through. "… gotta get going."

"Okay, well … See you around," she said. After thirty seconds or so, her voice sounded clearly. "Rats. He left."

"It's okay. We see him coming out," Beau told her. "He's getting into a black Tahoe."

The vehicle screeched lightly on the tarmac as Blackwood gunned it.

"Doesn't seem like a happy camper," Sam commented. "At least it's safe for you to come out now."

Cece appeared at the door a couple minutes later, just as Chief Rollie Benson pulled into the lot. Sam nudged Beau with her elbow, and they both saw Benson give Cece a long, appraising look.

# Chapter 22

A polka band occupied the bandstand, pumping out a thumping beat as the Cardwell group approached. They'd spent way too many hours delving into paperwork, trying to decipher Mark's notes and the files they'd brought home from their little foray into the abandoned warehouse. It was time to relax. And, for Beau, time to observe the locals who turned out for the big autumn picnic.

"Normally, it's held toward the end of October," Cecelia had told them this morning as they had their coffee. "But this year a big storm moved through right then. The town council decided to push it out a couple weeks, so here we are. The festivities start a little before noon."

At the park, the air was rich with the scent of barbecue and the sound of laughter. Cecelia nudged Sam toward the arts and crafts booths that lined the perimeter. "This is where I do half my Christmas shopping."

The two women moved in that direction, leaving Beau to decide whether he ought to have a beer this early in the day. He was staring at the menu at a little bratwurst stand when Olivia Sterling glided through the crowd. Her blonde hair was down in a more casual style and she wore jeans today, but still commanded attention with every step.

"Beau Cardwell, nice to see you here," Olivia greeted, extending a hand in a grip that was both firm and challenging.

"Olivia," Beau responded, matching her handshake. "Enjoying the festivities?"

Her gaze swept through the crowd. "What brings you here, Beau?"

"My cousin is attacking the gift booths. I'm just here for the food."

"Really." Olivia's voice carried some sort of nuance. "And how long do you plan to stay in Creston?"

He met her gaze firmly. "As long as it takes, I suppose."

"Well, if I can be of assistance …"

Was she actually being flirtatious, or was she probing to find out how much he knew? He wondered what she wanted from him.

"Oh, there's actually someone I know," he said, spotting Lucy Evergreen near the bandstand. "If you'll excuse me."

"Trouble?" Samantha sidled up to her husband, her gaze lingering on Olivia's retreating form.

"Maybe," Beau admitted. "I get the feeling she's playing chess while the rest of us are playing checkers."

"Then we'll need to think a few moves ahead," Samantha said, her eyes gleaming with resolve.

"I spotted Lucy a minute ago. Have you run into anybody else we know?"

"Not yet, but the day is young. Let's mingle."

The teacher had noticed them, as well, and she made her way over to say hello. "Having fun with those accounting entries?" she asked with a smile.

"Not really. I'm about to decide I'm a lot more comfortable on a horse than with a ledger book."

"I should have offered before, but if you'd like me to take a look, I'd be happy to help."

Noticing a flicker of relief on Beau's face, Sam piped up. "I'd say any and all assistance would be welcome right now."

"Let me know when you get ready to leave the picnic," Beau said, "and I'll run by Cece's house and get that book for you."

Lucy gave such an enthusiastic nod, Beau got the idea she was thrilled to contribute to the effort. He looked up to see another familiar figure approaching them.

"Lucy, do you know Aiden Wilder?" He performed a quick introduction, letting Lucy know Aiden was a private investigator who was also on the case.

A moment later, Cecelia rushed up to inform the ladies that one booth had the cutest handmade dolls. Sam perked up, obviously thinking of Ana's Christmas gift, and Lucy tagged along as they walked away.

Beau turned to Aiden. "Anything new on your end of things?"

"From my list of missing people, I did find a case of one woman who refused to leave town. She died two months later in a very suspicious accident. And probably the only reason I found that was because the accident didn't happen here in Creston. It was in Tulsa."

Beau cocked his head, questioning.

"This was a worker in the Sterling Microchips plant, a kind of spunky type according to her husband and friends. Mattie Brown. She told her husband she'd been threatened, that she needed to leave her job, and forget everything she ever saw there. She told him hell no, she was making good money, their kids were in a good school. She didn't want to leave. He was in agreement, so they stayed."

"But then …"

"Mattie went to Tulsa for her high school's twentieth class reunion. Late night, her car veers off the road and rolls over, and she's dead at the scene."

"Drinking?"

"No. Her blood alcohol content was practically zero. No one at the dinner had seen her drink anything but iced tea."

"So, a second vehicle?"

"Not that either. It simply appeared to be a one-car accident. The first impression was that she might have fallen asleep at the wheel, since this was a little ways out of town on a long stretch of road."

"I'm sensing a *but* …"

"The car was impounded and examined. Driver's window was down. There was a bullet lodged in the opposite side, in the passenger-side window frame."

"Someone took a shot at her."

"Yeah. The hole was fresh."

"If someone intended to kill her it would have definitely been investigated as a murder, but maybe they just wanted to frighten her into leaving."

"That's my guess." Aiden's gaze went across the park. "There's no way they could have been certain she would panic and swerve, rolling her car."

"How did the Tulsa police handle it?"

"They couldn't pin it on anyone. For all they know it might have been road rage. Those things happen. That's what they told her husband."

"You talked to him?"

"Yeah, for quite a while. As soon as he found out about the bullet, he took the hint and moved his kids away from Creston. They're in Oklahoma City and really don't want anyone here to know that."

"Got it."

"He said he was just thankful this happened in Tulsa jurisdiction, rather than here. He'd bet money that Rollie Benson would have found a way to lose the bullet and never tell anyone about it."

Beau looked at the faces in the crowd, seeing only a handful he recognized. "Let's take a walk while we talk. Okay, so the big question is, did Mr. Brown have any suspicions about who was so set on getting Mattie to quit her job?"

"We did get into that, yes. She didn't give names, but she'd told him there was 'this guy in accounting' who had asked questions around the floor—the manufacturing part of the plant."

"Mark?"

"She didn't say, but yeah, that would be my guess. She also mentioned a coworker on her shift, a guy who worked the quality control line, who seemed edgy all the time. Like he was doing something he shouldn't."

"I wonder who it was." Beau paused and scuffed the grass with the toe of his boot, thinking.

"We might be able to find out, if I could get hold of

employee records and shift assignments."

"I'll find out if Cecelia has any contacts in HR. If not, we met an older guy named Carson, head of monitoring the security videos. Seemed like a straight shooter. He might be able to request those records for us without drawing suspicion. Let me think on that."

They passed a huge metal cooker that was billowing smoke, fragrant with the scent of roasted meat and barbeque sauce.

"Here's where I stop," Aiden said with a wide grin. "This guy makes the absolutely best ribs, and I'd even debate anyone from St. Louis on that point."

"I'm going to find my wife and then I'll probably be right behind you."

"Get the coleslaw too. Yum." Aiden rubbed his stomach.

Beau laughed and turned to face the crowded interior of the park. Cecelia's short pixie haircut caught his attention and he spotted Sam with her. He walked toward them, noting that they both had tote bags hanging from their arms. "I see you've bought out all the vendors."

"And then some," Cece giggled. "Do you think we can find your truck and stow this stuff?"

He indicated the nearest side street, the only place he'd been able to find parking.

"I've got Christmas for Ana and Kelly, plus a little something for everyone at the bakery," Sam said as he unlocked the doors.

"Now we can eat," Cece declared. "I'm going for Max's ribs. It's the place near where you were standing when we found you."

Beau smiled. Apparently, this Max was well known

around here.

"You'd better grab us a seat," Cece said, waving toward the long tables under a big canopy. "We'll wait in line for the food."

There must have been eighty people in three long lines. Knowing he had some time, Beau pulled out his phone and called the main number for Sterling Microchips, assuming the huge place was a seven-day-a-week operation. Sure enough, someone answered. He asked for Carson in Security.

After a moment of uncertainty, the female voice came back. "I'm sorry, sir, he's not on duty today. Could someone else help you?"

"I'll just try again on Monday." Beau looked around. He spotted Olivia Sterling and Jason Blackwood, heads together, standing beside a booth that boasted hand carved wooden animals. Neither appeared to be shopping. After a full minute of what appeared to be intense conversation, they turned away, Jason slipping an arm lightly around her waist to guide her through the crowd.

Hmm. It fit with what Aiden had told him.

# Chapter 23

About twenty ribs later, the three of them sat back in a stupor. "Those were definitely the best ribs I've ever had," Beau told Sam and Cece. "And Aiden was right about the coleslaw too."

"I don't think you mentioned you had talked to Aiden." Sam licked her fingers and wiped them on a napkin.

"I'll fill you in at home."

Lucy Evergreen appeared at his side. "I see you discovered the most popular food here."

Beau nodded. "Ready for me to get that ledger for you?"

"I'm all set to leave. I can follow you, if you'd like."

Fifteen minutes later, standing in Cecelia's foyer, he handed the book over to the teacher. "As I said before, anything you can translate will be helpful to me. Even knowing what some of the accounting references stood for, I couldn't make much sense of it."

"I'll see what I can do. Did I happen to mention that solving puzzles and riddles is one of my favorite pastimes?"

Sam gave the older woman a hug. "I bet he wishes he'd asked you that sooner."

Lucy gave a thumbs-up and left.

Cece asked her guests if they'd like coffee, cold beverages, or naps. "If I lie down right now, I'll never get up again," Sam said. "How about a cup of tea? And I want to hear what Aiden had to say."

Beau filled them in on the whole story of the woman who died in the car accident because she probably knew too much about something that a shifty co-worker might have been doing down on the production floor of the plant.

"I'm trying to figure out how to learn who that worker is. Cece? Any ideas?"

She sipped from her mug and shook her head. "I know so few of the Sterling employees, especially in the manufacturing end of things."

"I'm trying to get hold of a man named Carson, in security. Sam and I talked to him yesterday."

"Oh, Carson Delaney? Ex-cop?"

"Yeah. I actually wasn't sure if Carson was his first or last name. That helps. You wouldn't by chance know how to reach him outside work?"

She nibbled at her lower lip for a moment. "Maybe. He and Mark went fishing once. Gosh, has to be three or four years ago. Mark probably has his number jotted down somewhere. I'll take a look in his desk."

She left the room, and Sam turned to Beau. "I notice you didn't make a big point of how that woman's car accident happened. But, honey, a bullet? What if somebody tries that with Cece? Or us?"

"Mattie Brown was warned and didn't leave. It doesn't justify what happened—*at all*. But the point being it wasn't a case of random potshots or road rage that could happen anywhere. Mark received a warning, probably, that beating. He kept pressing and we saw what happened. Cece hasn't received a warning, so she's probably safe. As long as we keep our investigation lowkey and don't start accusing until we have our facts lined up, I think we'll be fine."

"Makes sense. Okay."

"And we'll be ready to get all three of us to a safer place if somebody does try to scare us away." He took her hand and gave a gentle squeeze.

Cece came back to the kitchen, holding a yellow sticky note. "This is the number Mark had for Carson Delaney, and it's not one of the Sterling lines. So, it's probably either his cell or his home."

Beau called the number and the voice that answered was familiar to him. "Mr. Delaney, Beau Cardwell here. Are you free to speak for a couple minutes?" He began to pace as he talked, a habit Sam always teased him about.

"Sure, Beau, I'm at home by myself."

"We've received a tip that has me looking into one of the workers there. If I give you a date and time, can you find out who was working on the factory floor that shift?"

"You are in luck, Sheriff. I can do that. You've noticed the ID badges each employee wears? They have to scan them when they enter or leave the building, and again as they pass through to certain work areas. The production floor is one of those. If someone isn't authorized for that part of the facility, the doors stay locked."

"And those records are kept for some period of time?"

"At least a year. HR has that to fall back on in case of a time-sheet dispute or claim for vacation pay."

"Got it." Beau paused and stared out the window for a beat or two. "I'm looking at a female employee named Mattie Brown. She died in an accident about four months ago. I need to know who her coworkers were, particularly males who worked near her position on the production line."

"And I'm guessing you don't want to go straight to HR with this question."

"The fewer people who know we're asking, the better. I don't know who I can trust not to run straight to Jason Blackwood or Olivia Sterling with this."

"You're smart to consider that. Those two are really tight." Carson cleared his throat. "Mark Mitchell was a decent man and a friend. I feel guilty as hell that I didn't realize where we had a blind spot in that parking garage, and I'll do whatever I can to help find his killer."

Beau thanked him and let out a pent-up breath as he ended the call. At last—someone within Sterling Enterprises he felt he could trust.

He walked through the house, not finding the women in the kitchen or in Mark's study. From there, he wandered to the glass doors facing the back yard and saw them in chairs under the covered patio. The pool glistened beyond them, the setting sun casting a peachy glow over the property.

"Hey, you," Sam said, stretching a hand toward him and pulling him around to sit on the lounger next to hers.

"How did your call go?" Cecelia asked. Her eyes were half closed.

"I may have some names by tomorrow. I think Carson's

going to be a big help."

Cece rubbed her arms and pulled herself up from her chair. "The minute that sun went down it got downright chilly out here. Anyone up for some hot chocolate, or something stronger?"

They all trooped indoors and she led the way to the living room where she turned a knob to light the gas fireplace.

\* \* \*

Beau's predicted call from Carson Delaney came earlier than he could have guessed. He rolled over in bed to reach for the phone and saw the time was not quite seven.

"Sorry. I get to work at five and forget not everyone is up and at 'em this early."

"Perfectly fine, Carson. Have you found something?"

"I was able to pinpoint Mattie Brown's workstation and from that I learned who worked next to her on all sides. There's one man in particular I think might be of interest."

"I'd like to get a look at him and hopefully have a chance to ask some questions. Is he at work now?"

"His shift starts at eight. It's part of the reason I called so early."

"I'll be there."

Sam murmured something, half asleep, and he assured her she didn't need to tag along. By the time he finished his shower, she was fully awake. "I was thinking about going back to the library," she told him. "To see what Ethan may have come up with by now."

"Good plan. Let's keep each other posted."

He grabbed a muffin from a box of them on Cece's

kitchen counter and headed out to his truck. The computer chip manufacturing plant loomed ahead, all sleek glass and buzzing activity. Beau slipped in among a group of employees, badges clipped to their casual clothes. Carson had left a visitor badge for him at the front desk, and Beau spotted the older man near the stairs to the second floor mezzanine.

Olivia Sterling stood in the center of the mezzanine, like a general leading troops, watching her people arrive for work. She was a picture of corporate success, from her blonde bun to her sharp suit.

"Talk about presence," Beau whispered to the security man, eyes tracking Olivia's every move, studying Olivia's interactions with her employees. They were respectful, almost wary, around their CEO.

"Assertive doesn't even begin to cover it."

He wondered if that meant she was assertive enough to order a murder, but knew he'd need more than observing a strong personality to make that stick.

He turned back to Carson. "So, about that worker you mentioned? Have you seen him come through?"

Carson consulted the iPad he held. "He arrived twenty minutes ago, a little early for his shift. Let's check out the production floor."

The security man led the way. Taking the elevator to the third floor, then following a series of winding hallways, they came to a glassed-in observation deck. Below, they could see the massive machinery and busy employees dressed in white coveralls, paper booties, and paper caps to cover their hair. Men with facial hair had additional coverage there.

"See that guy?" Carson's voice was barely audible over

the hum of equipment.

He nodded toward the end of the line where a man hunched over the moving conveyor belt, his fingers picking chips off the belt, setting certain ones on a microscope stand, letting others pass through.

"Name's Johnny Smith. I did a little digging. He grew up here in town. Dad was a farmer who had a hard time keeping up and ended up losing everything in the last recession. When the plant opened, Johnny got a job and worked his way up to what he does now, inspecting chips as they reach the end of the line. Quality control. What he earns here is probably the most anyone in his family ever made."

"Is there any way he can cheat at the job?" Beau chuckled at himself. "I should ask, in what way can a person cheat at that job?" People could find ways to cheat at anything, he'd discovered.

Carson shrugged. "I'm not familiar enough with the various processes down there on the floor, so I honestly don't know the answer to that."

Johnny Smith turned and threw a quick glance over his shoulder, almost as if he knew he was being watched. Beau stepped back from the glass, now determined he would speak with the man.

# Chapter 24

After Beau left, Sam couldn't get back to sleep. Cecelia had apparently gone to an early meeting, and Sam found herself alone in the big house. Alone for the first time in days, and the silence felt good. She rummaged in the fridge and made herself an omelet with an egg and a variety of vegetables.

Sitting at the breakfast counter, she realized the house was too quiet. She missed home—the ever-presence of having dogs around, knowing Beau and the horses were somewhere on the property. She could understand why Cecelia was considering selling the massive house. It really did become somewhat eerie for one person.

"Well, there are things to do and people to talk to," she said aloud to the houseplant on the windowsill.

Placing her plate and utensils in the dishwasher, she

grabbed a jacket and headed to the garage, thankful Cece had left her with keys to the Toyota and free rein to use it.

"Ethan, hello?" Sam called out as she walked into the library.

He emerged from a back room and smiled. "Hi, Samantha. How's it going?"

"I just thought I'd circle back to what we were talking about the other day, see if you'd had any further luck in finding out what our mysterious JCI stands for."

He perched on the edge of his desk, his hands clasped tightly, shaking his head. "No, but funny you should use that word. I actually searched for the term 'Creston mysteries' at one point."

"Ooh, interesting. What came up?"

"Creston's had its share of crime stories, as it turns out," Ethan began, warming to his subject. "There was a case of embezzlement, town funds gone missing. There have even been a couple of murders before this latest one, way back in time. But nothing I could find—mysterious or not—that tied in with what you're looking for."

"You're quite the historian, Ethan." She gave him an encouraging smile. "Since I was here last time, we came across some information on a business that was here in town—Cormorant. They manufactured packaging materials. It appears they left suddenly, not even bothering to pack up their files or sell off their equipment."

He scratched his head, making his unruly hair go even wilder. "I remember that name, do not remember hearing what happened to the place. That's interesting that they didn't take anything with them."

"I gather they shut down about the time Sterling Microchips decided Creston would be their headquarters.

I'm curious whether those two events could be related."

"No idea about that. And I'm not even sure how one would go about searching for such a thing. Computer results don't tend to point out coincidences."

Sam sighed. "Yeah, I was afraid of that."

Another patron walked in just then, an elderly woman with an armload of books to return. Sam moved away to give Ethan a chance to talk with her. On the shelving to her right were bound editions of the local Creston newspaper, apparently a weekly based on the dates on the spines. She traced the titles until she found the one for the week when Mark was killed. But when she opened it, this was the same issue she'd already found in her research.

On a whim, she looked for the date when Mattie Brown's accident happened. There was a front page writeup about it, and she read the article carefully. It contained only what the official investigation had noted: one-car accident, cause unknown. No mention of the bullet hole or the possibility that Mattie's death had been engineered to look accidental.

By the time she'd finished reading the articles and replaced the bound volumes on the shelves, several more patrons had come in and Ethan's attention was divided many ways. Sam gave a little wave goodbye and headed out, frustrated at the lack of answers.

* * *

Beau thanked Carson Delaney for the information and turned to leave the man to his work. He'd almost reached the front desk to turn in his visitor badge when his phone rang. He set the badge on the desk and kept walking, touching his screen to take Lucy's call.

"You're not in school today?" he asked with a smile in his voice.

"On a break between class periods. I had the best time last night, going through that journal of Mark's. There are clues galore in there."

"Wow, I'm impressed. All I got from it was a headache."

"If you're interested in taking a teacher to lunch, I can go over what I've found. My lunch break is at eleven-thirty."

"You got it. I'll be in front of the school then."

He texted Sam as soon as the call ended, asking if she would be able to join them. Eight minutes later, the SUV pulled into the school parking lot next to his truck. It was 11:14.

Sam climbed into his truck and turned toward him. "So, what's the lunch plan?"

"Figured we'd play it by ear. Shouldn't have any trouble getting a table this early."

"Let's think of somewhere that would be quiet enough to talk and private enough where no one will overhear what she has to say."

He glanced around. The Indian summer weather was still holding. "Warm enough to eat outside, if you'd like."

"I'll run and get us some sandwiches at the deli and meet you two at the park." She was already halfway out of the truck.

"Good plan …" he called as she got in her vehicle.

The concrete picnic benches were a little chilly, but they were so eager to hear what Lucy had discovered that no one noticed.

"Chicken salad, egg salad, or ham and cheese," Sam said, pulling wrapped packets from the bag. "And I decided to play it safe with iced tea all around."

"So, Lucy, you said you were able to read Mark's notes?" Beau asked, biting into his ham sandwich.

The older woman chuckled. "Mark took my shorthand class in school. I could read it perfectly."

"Shorthand? I thought that was a lost art," Sam said, remembering back to her early days when working in an insurance office. Even then, the quick method of taking notes was pretty much out of fashion.

"It is. And I didn't actually teach an entire class on it. We'd do a little week-long unit, more of a fun thing for the kids to get a taste of the *olden days*, as they said it."

"Well, apparently it came in handy for Mark in keeping a journal no one else could decipher." Beau caught her look. "Anyone but you. Thank goodness."

"Several pages in the book are devoted to observations Mark made while watching the chip assembly part of the factory. And what led him there was that he was noticing discrepancies in the paperwork. The number of chips manufactured didn't match up with what was shipped and billed to customers."

"Maybe due to quality control, some of the chips being rejected?" Sam suggested. She was thinking in bakery terms. Some of the cookies and muffins just weren't good looking enough to put out for the customers.

Lucy nodded. "There is that. He mentions the reject-bin, although I'm not sure that's the official name for it in their corporate lingo. Even taking those into account, the numbers should add up. Mark noticed they didn't. And the numbers weren't small. There were big discrepancies, into the thousands of chips."

"Wow. I'm guessing that's a lot of money." Beau

reached for the bag of chips.

"That's in another section of the journal," Lucy confirmed. "He's got some notes, and also refers to an XLS. That's a spreadsheet, which he must have been keeping on the computer."

"We'll see if we can find that."

Sam set down her iced tea, getting excited. "So, if Mark got that far with his evidence, he must have also been looking to figure out who was doing this … this pilfering."

"He was careful," Lucy said. "I'll give him that. A lot of what are probably people's names are only listed by their initials. I've made a list." She drew out a small slip of paper with only about a half-dozen sets of initials.

"MB—that's probably Mattie Brown," Sam said, a sick feeling forming in her gut.

"The one I found repeatedly, especially in the part where he's watching the manufacturing process, is a JS. I don't know who that is." Lucy seemed disappointed. "Doesn't match with Jason Blackwood. I guess with a full list of the employees, it would be easy enough to find."

"I think I know," Beau told them. "Just this morning, Carson Delaney in security pointed out a worker on the assembly line, a Johnny Smith. This Smith worked next to Mattie, where their jobs are to inspect the finished chips under a microscope."

"An easy place to reject chips that are actually perfectly fine, if no one else is double checking …" Sam's mind was reeling.

"Exactly. Rejected chips go into the bin, maybe the bin gets stashed away where it can be overlooked for a few days." Beau tapped his fingers on the concrete table. "Those things are tiny. A whole lot of them could leave the plant in the bottom of a lunchbox or in someone's pockets."

"But surely the company has safeguards in place for that." Lucy seemed concerned. "I've got a friend who has worked in places where the women were required to carry clear plastic purses, where employees had to walk through scanners at the end of the day. Inventory doesn't just walk out the door."

"We may not know the *how*, but it seems Mark was definitely onto the fact that something like this was happening."

Sitting next to Lucy, Sam glanced over at the journal pages. "Did you make it through all of his notes?"

"Once I found out what I've just told you, I only got around to a cursory glance through the rest of it. Want me to keep trying?"

"Yes, please," Beau said. "I'll take this list of initials and see if I can enlist Carson's help in figuring out who they are and what their job duties entail."

Lucy glanced at her watch. "Much as I'd like to stick with this all afternoon, I really need to get back to school. Can I get back to you in a day or two?"

# Chapter 25

Beau sat in his truck, parked in the shadow of a billboard, a quarter of a mile outside the gates to Sterling Enterprises. It was late afternoon, and the view of the garage exit at Sterling told him it was quitting time for the day shift. Vehicles flowed out to the long driveway and onto the highway in a steady stream.

He raised his binoculars. Carson had given him the make and model of Johnny Smith's ride, a pickup truck with a red camper shell. Easy to spot. He also had the address of Smith's home, but wasn't certain the man would go directly there. And Beau wanted to catch him before he had a chance to relax and settle in.

Here came the truck. Beau started his engine and pulled onto the four-lane highway slightly ahead of his target, then dropped back, letting Smith pass him so he got a good look at the driver. Yep, he thought, that's the one. A mile later, Smith pulled into the lot at a convenience store and Beau parked directly in front of a coin laundry next door. He slouched in his seat, hoping his quarry hadn't spotted him, watching until the man came out five minutes later with a six-pack of Bud under one arm. He walked directly to his truck and got in, not looking in either direction.

Good.

The route led into a nice neighborhood, with fairly new tract housing and immature trees. From the end of the street, Beau watched as Smith pulled into the driveway of the third house on the left. He moved out of sight as the driver's door started to open. Circling the block, Beau drew to the curb two houses away, got out and locked his truck, and walked up.

Smith had set his six-pack on a chair on the front porch and was coiling a garden hose around a hanger mounted to the wall.

"Johnny Smith?" Beau called out.

The man's head shot up, on alert. "Yeah? Do I know you?"

"You work at Sterling, right?" Beau stood squarely on the short sidewalk that blocked Smith from running to his truck. He would have to drop the hose, find his house key, and get the door open fast, or he'd have to stand there and talk.

"We're looking into Mark Mitchell's death, just talking with folks who might have spoken with him right before or might have been around the night he was attacked in the garage there."

Smith shrugged and turned his attention back to the garden hose. "Not me."

"But you knew Mark, right? He'd asked some questions

about the shipping and billing documents of certain chips. We know he talked with Mattie Brown about it, and she worked right next to you on the line."

"I don't know nothin' about any documents. I inspect the chips. That's it." His words were confident but his eyes darted about, not meeting Beau's steady gaze.

"A lot of chips have defects, don't they? Must be quite a challenging job to spot the bad ones."

"Look, mister …"

"Sheriff."

Beau realized his mistake a nano-second later. Smith dropped the hose and stood with his hands on his hips.

"I got no duty to talk to you, whoever you are. Ever'body at the plant got interviewed when Mitchell got killed. I told the cops all I knew, which was nothin'. I can get me a lawyer."

"No need to do that," Beau said, keeping his body language casual. "I'm just working for his widow, trying to give her some peace of mind, hoping we can figure out who killed her husband. Thought you might have seen something. That's all."

"Well, I didn't." At least his stance had relaxed.

"Right. Well, if you think of anything, maybe something you forgot to tell the local police, I'd appreciate a call."

"I won't be calling. I said I don't know nothing."

"Fine." Beau turned to leave, watching from the corner of his eye.

Smith kicked the half-coiled garden hose aside, fished around in his jeans pocket for a keyring, and picked up his beers. By the time Beau was fifty feet away he heard the front door of the house close with a bang.

Rattled. Huh. At least he'd diffused the moment when

Smith looked as if he might resort to fists. He walked back to his truck, backed it to the nearest corner, and waited. Who knew if Smith was inside right now, getting some kind of instructions, or if he'd just kicked off his boots and flopped into a chair with a cold one.

After twenty minutes without an appearance, he assumed the latter. He phoned Sam.

* * *

Sam put the finishing touches on a salad, while Cecelia pulled the lasagna pan from the oven. "Um, that smells *so* good. When Beau called, I told him dinner would be ready as soon as he can get here."

"I'll put the garlic toast under the broiler once he's settled in."

"I'm eager to hear whether he learned anything from this guy he was going to talk to, the one from the production part of Sterling. You're sure Mark never mentioned the name Johnny Smith?"

"Not to me. Like I told y'all, he never much talked about work."

The sound of a key in the front door got their attention, and Beau walked into the kitchen a few seconds later.

"Smells good in here." He gave Sam a kiss on the forehead.

"Wash up. It'll be on the table in less than five minutes," Cece told him.

As they scooped lasagna and salad onto their plates, Beau related the unproductive encounter with Johnny Smith. "I could have handled it better, maybe waited until he had a beer or two in him. I don't know … even then he might not have opened up. The guy is hinky. I saw it even while Carson and I watched him on the job."

"Sounds like he's hiding something."

"I'm leaning more toward him doing something devious with the rejected chips, not so much that he had anything to do with Mark's death."

"Which fits with what Lucy told us at lunch, what she read in Mark's journal." Sam broke a corner off her garlic toast and nibbled at it.

"Still, don't y'all think both things are related? My husband knew something was up. Maybe this Smith guy figured it out, told somebody else Mark was onto their scheme, whatever that was?"

Beau nodded slowly. "We can't rule anything out. It's just frustrating."

Sam thought of something. "When I was at the library this morning, I discovered they have a newspaper archive. I looked up the article about Mattie Brown's accident. The local paper reported pretty much what the official line was, no mention of the bullet hole."

"So, no one shared that tidbit with them," Beau suggested. "Which reminds me, speaking of accidents … That newspaper we found out at the Cormorant factory, the one that mentioned Taos … While I was sitting out there waiting for Smith this afternoon, it came to me that the vehicle accident near Taos was one of Cormorant's trucks."

"So, do you think that's all the connection there is?" Sam asked. "The company kept an old, yellowed clipping just because one of their vehicles was involved? Maybe I should take another look after dinner."

"I'm guessing that's all it was. Still, I'm going to keep my eyes open. You know how coincidences bother me."

"Well, I for one, need a break from all this," Cece announced. "There's Cherry Garcia ice cream in the freezer and I'm suggesting we each have a bowl and watch a movie tonight. And it needs to be something lighthearted and funny."

Sam studied her face as she cleared the dishes and carried them to the kitchen sink. Beau's poor cousin had been through so much. It showed.

* * *

Beau rolled over in bed and put his arm around Sam's waist. She'd been restless ever since she fell asleep, hours ago. Probably too much rich food topped with ice cream. His touch startled her awake and she sat up.

"JCI—I think I know what it is!" Her hair spiked wildly around her head and in the dim moonlight through the window he saw excitement in her expression.

"Sam … honey, I think you're dreaming."

"I was, but not now. I had this weird sort of … I don't know … epiphany. It's Cormorant. JCI. Remember? The guy's name was Jay Cormorant. Jay Cormorant Industries. That's who Mark paid the thousand dollars to."

Beau stared at the ceiling. Could it be true? They hadn't made any other connection with those initials.

Once Sam shared her idea, she relaxed and almost immediately fell into a quiet sleep. Beau lay there, going back over everything they'd learned. He would need to update his notes but didn't want to wake Sam by getting out of bed. He drifted off, just before dawn.

When his phone rang at 8:24 he reached for it, then jolted awake when he saw the name on the screen.

"Carson. What's up?"

"Johnny Smith didn't show up for work this morning. When his badge didn't get scanned, I called down to his shift supervisor. He never called in either."

"I'll go over to his house," Beau said, swinging his legs over the edge of the bed, reaching for the jeans and shirt he'd draped over a chair last night. "I could use some backup, if you can come."

"I'll be there."

Beau swished mouthwash and barely combed his hair before heading out. Sam was still sleeping peacefully and there was no way he was going to disturb her. He jumped in his truck and pulled up in front of Smith's home barely ten minutes after Carson's call. When he realized the man was loading something into the back of his camper shell, he blocked the driveway.

"Johnny, what's up?" He tried for a casual tone, but wasn't sure he pulled it off.

The wiry man stared at him. "Going camping. Not that it's any of your business."

A Ford SUV pulled up in front of the house. Carson and another man Beau recognized from the security team got out. The two approached, spreading out to cover all sides. Smith gave a nervous glance toward his open garage door, but the third man stood there.

"Carson, Mr. Smith here says he's packing for a camping trip."

"On a Tuesday? And it seems you failed to let your supervisor know about this."

"So? I forgot, okay. Arrest me." He seemed to think

better of that last bit. "I mean, there's nothing illegal about that."

Carson held out a placating hand. "No, there's not, Johnny. We just got concerned when you didn't report." Then he moved in a little closer. "But—you gotta admit this is not good timing."

Smith shifted uneasily.

Beau took the bad-cop role. "Yesterday I asked you some questions about a murder, some questions about chips that went missing from the factory. Today, you're packing up. You're in this thing deep, Johnny, and that joke of a local police chief isn't going to cover your butt this time. We've got county and state lawmen on it now."

Johnny's eyes shifted between Carson and the other Sterling employee, and he tried one more time to bluster. "These guys? They got no clout."

Beau pulled his phone from his back pocket. "Oh, it'll only take two seconds before I can have them on the way."

"Talk to us, man," Carson said. "Just tell us who's behind the racket with the chips."

Smith's eyes went wide and he frantically shook his head. "No way."

"Okay, then, without naming names, tell us how it works."

When Smith clamped his mouth shut, Beau stepped in again. "We've probably already got most of it. Your job is to reject faulty chips. You put good ones into the reject bin, they don't go into Sterling's inventory, and instead you're selling them to someone else." He gazed toward the man's home. "Pretty nice house you got here. Did you afford this on your hourly wage?"

Carson picked up the thread. "You know, I can easily

access your records and find out exactly how much money you take home every month. It isn't classified or anything."

The third man, standing behind Smith, made a slight move, scuffling his feet.

"Okay, okay." Johnny Smith's mouth trembled and he ran a hand through his hair. "You've got most of it right. I'm being paid to toss good chips out."

"And then?"

"And then I don't know. The bin I put them in goes away sometime after my shift. I ain't got no say over that, and I turn my head."

"Who gives the orders?" Carson wanted to know.

Smith shook his head slowly. "No idea."

"Oh, come on." Beau was getting impatient. "Somebody told you to do this."

"I got a note one day, said if I'd see to it that a hundred good chips went into this special bin, I'd see an extra thousand dollars in my pay that week."

"When was this?"

"Started about two years ago. Every week, there was more money." He raised his chin, defying them. "Hey, I gotta make a decent living too."

"And in those two years, you didn't have contact with an actual person. Seriously?"

"Nope. Okay, there was this once when a guy I didn't know, somebody from admin, came up and gave me a pat on the back and a 'good job' kind of comment."

"Any idea who he worked for?" Carson asked.

"Somebody higher than him. Think I'm gonna name somebody and lose my job?"

Beau held his phone up again, his thumb poised above the screen.

"Okay, maybe somebody in Mr. Blackwood's department. But you never heard that from me."

Carson sighed, debating. "All right. I'm going back to the office and I'll tell your supervisor I checked in on you and you're definitely ill. Don't come back until next Monday. And don't leave town. This truck had better be in this driveway any time I come cruising past here." He turned, and the others followed.

Smith went into the garage and the door began to roll down.

"Do you think he's right about Jason Blackwood being involved in this?" Beau asked quietly as they walked to the street.

"I don't know. Between you and me, I don't exactly trust the man's scruples. But I'm not ready to voice that at work. He signs my paycheck too." Carson met his gaze firmly. "However, if you want to pursue that line, and if you get enough evidence to make it stick, I'll step forward and repeat what I heard here."

"One other thing comes to mind. The first time I went out to Sterling—and I really hadn't even begun asking the tough questions—someone stuck a tracker on my truck. Any ideas about that?"

"The two big guys who sit out in the booth at the entry gate, they don't report to me. Their jobs fall under admin."

"So, Jason Blackwood?"

A nod. "You didn't hear it from me, okay?"

# Chapter 26

Sam thumbed through the papers scattered across the kitchen table, her brow furrowed in concentration.

Beau sat opposite her, a steaming mug of coffee in hand. "I was ready for this," he said, savoring the aroma and reaching for the plate of scones she'd set out. "Can't believe I rushed out this morning without my waker-upper."

Sam laughed. "I was wondering. I never heard you leave, and Cece said she didn't either."

"Where is she, anyway?"

"Another meeting with Melissa, something to do with the hospital's annual Christmas party for the kids."

"She sure stays busy." He buttered a scone and looked like he was ready to pop a bite of it into his mouth. "But I suppose she needs that. Her first holiday season without

Mark. It'll be rough."

"Maybe we should invite her to have Thanksgiving, and maybe Christmas, with us."

"We'll ask. She's got other people, too. Her younger brother moved to Kansas City and has a big family with kids. And their mother is still alive. Almost ninety now, I think. She's in an assisted living place near Kyle."

"Okay. At least let her know she's welcome." Sam turned back to the papers, pieces gleaned from the folders they'd brought back from the Cormorant warehouse.

Ever since her nighttime 'revelation' that the mysterious JCI could stand for Jay Cormorant Industries, she'd been looking for some evidence to corroborate that. So far, nothing. She'd begun to think maybe it was a silly dream, one that meant her brain was only trying to fit a random set of clues together.

"Help me think this through, Beau. I'm trying to review what we've got and I have no idea what to believe, or who we can trust." Samantha mused aloud, breaking the silence.

"Agreed. Trust is a luxury we can't afford right now," Beau said, setting down his mug with a clink. "Jason Blackwood's too sharp, Mark's notes are still too secretive, and we've probably learned all we can from that factory worker."

"Jason's ambition could be a motive," Samantha suggested, tapping on Mark's files. "But ambition doesn't always lead to murder."

"True. He could be completely up to his neck in the theft of the computer chips, but not involved in Mark's murder at all. I wish we knew who was on the other end of the thefts, who was buying them."

"And I'd love to know if Olivia Sterling is even aware. It could be that Mark was putting together a report, planning to take it to her and let the shakeups come from her office." Sam walked over to the coffee machine and brewed another cup for herself.

"I think Olivia's hiding something behind that CEO veneer," Beau stated, leaning against the countertop. "She's … I don't know. Either she was outrageously flirting with me the other day at the picnic, or she's up to something else."

"Maybe both." Sam gave a quirk of a smile. "I get the sense the factory guy's jittery, like he's waiting for the other shoe to drop."

"Seems we're playing a game where everyone's bluffing," Beau said, the light from the kitchen window casting shadows across his face.

"Then let's call their bluff." Samantha's eyes reflected the same unwavering resolve. "Certain corporate records are public. Let's see what we can learn about both Sterling and Cormorant. Maybe two and two really will equal four, once we get it put together. Go get Mark's computer and bring it here. I'll use mine, and we can both do some searches at the same time."

"Good plan. Um, if you coach me through how to read a financial report."

Beau clicked his way through a bunch of reports, a furrow etching deeper into his brow with each page. "Sterling's financials seem a little shaky," he said, showing his screen to Sam.

She crinkled her nose as she tried to make sense of the page, a profit and loss report that came as part of the corporation's annual report. "Looks like the year-over-year numbers are down."

"And look at this other," he said, scrolling to another page. "It's the comparison of the two previous years.

Definitely down."

"Which coincides with what that Smith guy told you about when he was approached to start stealing the chips."

"Right. Inventory that goes missing costs a company a lot of money. Am I right?"

"You are definitely getting it, Sheriff Cardwell." She planted a kiss on the side of his neck. "And talk about a motive. Money has a way of souring sweet deals."

"True, but is it enough to kill for?" Beau leaned back, running a hand across his jaw.

"What about the factory guy?" Sam tapped her pen impatiently on the table. "He was gullible enough to succumb to theft. Do you think he'd follow through and kill if someone told him to?"

"I doubt it. He's kind of a weasel, but I didn't sense a lot of anger there. There usually has to be some level of rage for a person to kill another."

"Still, we can't ignore anyone." Beau tapped the table. "Mark knew things, Sam. Things someone might kill to keep quiet. Fear or jealousy can be motivators, too."

"Knowledge is power," she agreed, nodding slowly. "But power isn't always the endgame. Sometimes it's personal."

"Which brings us back to either Jason or Olivia. They have the means, maybe even the motive, but also the most to lose. Can we tie either of them to the crime scene at the time of the murder?" Beau sighed. "Establishing alibis is something the local police investigation should have covered, but I'd bet Benson didn't do it thoroughly. I still wish I could get hold of those files."

"Loose threads," Samantha murmured. "Maybe if we pull, we'll see what unravels."

"Carefully though." He pushed Mark's computer away and leaned back in his chair, looking toward Sam. "What about Cormorant? What did you find there?"

"Not a lot, unfortunately. They shut down so long ago that there are no financial records. I'm guessing the old rule about keeping things for seven years has passed. There's still the book and file with Project Phoenix on them. I'm going to dig back into that a bit. In fact …" She began a new search on her laptop.

Beau's phone rang and he saw it was Lucy Greenwood. "Hey, how's our favorite teacher and puzzle solver?"

"Oh, Beau, you silly thing. But you're close. I have transcribed a bit more of Mark's journal. The word embezzlement has come up. Does that fit with what you're looking for?"

"Embezzlement? At Sterling Microchips?"

Sam raised her head, hearing the word. Beau placed the phone on speaker when Lucy spoke again. "It doesn't say. There's just 'embezzlement' and a question mark. Like he was planning to check it out, perhaps."

"But it doesn't mention anyone by name, somewhere in the same sentence or paragraph?"

"No. I'm not even sure why I bothered you with it until I knew more. Just hoping it would be of help."

"Hey, at this point, everything helps in some way. We've got so many unanswered questions, we're not sure where to turn next. If you're okay with it, just keep going. And feel free to bring up anything that might be a clue. Anytime."

When the call ended, Sam got Beau's attention. "This is the second time I've heard something about embezzlement. I came across something at the library, and now I don't remember the details. Ethan did tell me there was a trial, a case of embezzlement by one of the town officials, I think he said."

"Related to either of these companies we're looking at?"

She shook her head. "Forget it. I can't think how that could possibly be tied to anything at Sterling, something Mark would have noted."

He set his phone down and stared out the window, pondering.

"Beau, do you ever get the feeling we're chasing our tails, that we're nowhere close to a solution?"

"Darlin' it happens a lot. Nearly every case I've worked has that element, a darkness before the dawn kind of feeling. We'll get there."

"But not every case gets solved. That's why there are cold case files that sit around forever."

"I'm not thinking that way yet, Sam. I see a whole lot of leads, some of them puzzling, but I think we're on track with something."

"Just be careful, Beau. Mark was onto something too, and look what happened."

"Do you want to go home? Cause I'm not willing to put our lives on the line for this. If something's telling you to quit, then we will."

She closed the lid of her laptop and rubbed her temples. "No, I'm just tired."

"Would an ice cream help?" His blue eyes twinkled as he said it. "I happen to know where they make the best hot fudge sundae in this town."

"If you're asking me out on a date, it's a great big *yes!*" She tamped the papers into a neat stack and grabbed her jacket.

Sam knew she was enchanted when she saw the cute

little mock-Victorian shop with white siding, purple trim, and an ice cream sundae in the logo. Krystal's Kandy Kove.

"There's candy too?"

"Oh, I didn't mention that Krystal's grandmother passed down her recipes for homemade fudge?"

Inside, the old-fashioned ice cream shop lived up to its exterior appearance and reputation. Lace curtains framed beveled glass in the door and above the windows. Stained glass fixtures hung above the marble-topped tables with their cane back chairs. Beau stepped forward and ordered two hot fudge sundaes and a pound of assorted fudge, boxed to take home.

"So, this place was here when you were a kid?" Sam asked when the silver dish arrived with rich vanilla ice cream, smothered in hot fudge sauce, sprinkled with chopped pecans, whipped cream, and a cherry on the top.

"This place has been here since God was a kid. Everyone in a hundred-mile radius knows about Krystal's."

Sam dug in, savoring the combination of flavors, as he went on to tell the story of the Depression-era woman who risked the family's supply of eggs and cream on a batch of homemade vanilla, opened a tiny stand on this corner of the main square, and was sold out of the small cups of the creamy treat within the hour. The next day she bought more ingredients and made a double batch. And so on.

"By the time World War II started, she had GIs driving out here from all over the state, just to get a chocolate sundae before they shipped out. When they came back and the baby boom started, the line was out the door and down the street most of the time."

"And her name was Krystal?"

"Actually, her name was Mary. She always wanted a daughter and planned to name her Krystal, very specifically to be spelled with a K. That never happened, but she made it a stipulation of her will that a granddaughter in each generation should carry that name. It worked. Her boys produced little girls, and there's been a Krystal in the family ever since. And the shop has stayed in the family all this time too."

Sam set down her spoon and peered into the fudge box.

"They added candy to the offerings sometime in the 1950s. And that's all I know."

"Well, you have certainly brightened my day with this treat and the story, Sheriff Cardwell." She reached across the table and took his hand.

"You keep calling me sheriff. Are you wishing I'd get off my horse and go back to work?"

She shook her head. "I think you should follow your heart, Beau. Whatever floats your boat, as they say."

He laughed out loud. "Well, we shall see about that. Not to put a damper on things, but this case we're on now has reminded me how it's not always easy."

"And that's precisely why I would never push." She gave a little smile. "We'll just see."

A set of tiny bells above the door tinkled as it opened, letting in a rush of the crisp November air. Olivia Sterling walked in, her business suit as flawless as ever, her heels clicking on the hex-tile flooring.

"Well, Beau and ... Sam, right? Interesting to see you both here."

"I guess we like ice cream as well as the next person," he said, rising as she approached their table.

"Join us, if you'd like," Sam invited.

"Oh, I'm just going to get the smallest cone," Olivia said, turning toward the sales counter.

*Of course you are.* Sam kept that thought to herself, eyeing Olivia's narrow hips and waist. Still, once she had her cone in hand, the executive came and sat in the chair to Sam's right.

Beau cleared his throat and took a sip of his water. "Since we have you outside your office setting, Olivia, can I ask a question? It's business related and I don't mean to ruin a social moment …"

"Oh, just come out with it, Beau. Haven't you learned by now that a business owner is always on duty?" But she said it with a smile.

"You know we're looking into Mark Mitchell's death. And in the course of that we've come across some notes that indicate there may have been some thefts of inventory."

Sam noticed how he muted the revelation with 'may have been' and a soft tone of voice.

Olivia's gaze sharpened but she didn't speak.

"You don't seem surprised."

"If you're halfway decent at your job, I assume you've seen our latest corporate reports and know our profits are down," she said. "Where are you going with this?"

"Okay, I'll be blunt. Could Jason Blackwood be involved?"

"Jason? He's my second in command, and we're … well, he'd *like us to be* more romantically involved."

"And you trust him implicitly?"

"Well, I didn't say that." She took a final chomp on the cone and dropped her wadded napkin on the table. "But I didn't say that I *don't* trust him. What makes you ask?"

"We've found an employee who admits to being in on it. This person hasn't named Jason either, but—"

"So, you're just fishing." She stood, sending her chair scraping on the tile. "I don't much like fishing."

"It's a little more than merely fishing," he said. "But at this point I'm just letting the CEO of a successful company know that there's some embezzling going on under your roof. That's all."

"Olivia," Sam said softly, "if you have any ideas and would like to help us uncover this … It's really in your company's best interests."

Olivia softened, brushing back a stray hair where none had escaped from her precise bun. "I appreciate your kind thoughts, and I will … take precautions."

They watched her walk out, spine straight, steps deliberate.

"We did what we could," Sam said, scraping the last of the cream from her bowl.

"Yep, we did. Ready to go?" Beau picked up the fudge box and they headed for the door.

Outside, they spotted a figure in blue next to his truck. Olivia.

"I'm sorry. I …" a reddish tinge came into her eyelids "… it's been a strange morning. I shouldn't have blown off your offer. Yes, I would like to find out what's going on with the inventory shortages. Whatever you can tell me would be most appreciated."

"Even if it involves Jason?" Sam asked.

"I guess I have to say, especially if it involves Jason. He wants me to marry him. I need to know that man thoroughly." She took a deep, shaky breath. "I don't suppose I need to tell you that I don't want you going straight to him with what I just said."

Sam made a zipping motion across her lips, and Beau reached out and shook Olivia's hand.

# Chapter 27

Cecelia was home when they arrived back at her place. "Well. I had an interesting morning," she said when they walked through the front door. She was standing with her hands on her hips, staring toward the front windows.

"I'm guessing by your tone that *interesting* was not especially good?" Sam questioned.

"Oh, you got that right." She dropped her arms and faced them. "Melissa and I were having a productive meeting, talking about the hospital board's sponsorship of the Christmas party next month, when … out comes this little bombshell. Apparently, the local gossip mill has it that Mark and I were in on some kind of racket out at Sterling."

"What? What kind of *racket?*" Concern etched Sam's face.

"Various theories abound. Mark was skimming money

and I was helping him hide it in offshore accounts … We traveled so frequently—always first class or by private jet—because he was receiving hush money from someone out there …" Her face crumpled. "I can't believe our friends and neighbors would be talking this way."

"And it was Melissa who told you about this?" Beau had begun pacing the width of the living room.

"Yes. But I don't blame her. She was nearly in tears as she told me what she'd been hearing."

"Hearing from whom?"

"Well, now that it's all over town, supposedly, it's hard to say who started it. Melissa said she heard it from Ethan. The ladies book club seems to have been reading too many espionage thrillers."

"So, it's purely gossip," Sam said, picturing a group of old women with nothing better to do.

"Of course it's only gossip, but in a town this size that kind of thing can ruin you. Melissa suggested I might want to step away from the hospital board for a while, until it blows over. She was gentle about it, but I tell you, this hurts."

Sam spotted the box of fudge she'd set on a side table in the foyer. "Maybe we could all use a cup of tea."

"Hon, this isn't something tea and fudge can fix," Beau said.

"Sorry. I know."

"They're all saying the whole thing, our having money all of a sudden, and everything—it's just too convenient."

"Convenient doesn't mean complicit," Beau reminded. "What we have to do is work faster and dig deeper. Thank goodness we have reliable allies like Aiden and Lucy."

"And Melissa. She didn't have to tell me what the town

is saying about me, but she did." Cece picked up the fudge box and headed toward the kitchen, filling the kettle and pulling out her teabag collection. "Hey, how about if we get Lucy into that book club, and ask Ethan to keep his ears open during their meetings. I'd bet the two of them would help us squash those ugly rumors."

"I like that," Sam said.

She looked around and didn't see Beau. When she found him, he was standing in the center of the living room, a look of consternation on his face. "Honey, what is it?"

"I can't believe I've jumped this far into this case without doing the most basic of basic investigatory work."

She shrugged—what?

"We haven't been to the crime scene."

* * *

The parking garage was deep in shadows when they followed Carson out of the elevator. He showed them the discreet cameras mounted on support pillars.

"There are two parking levels, and both have the same setup," he said.

He turned right and led the way to a space where little light penetrated. On the wall beside it stood a door marked Custodial Staff.

"This is where Mark was killed." He pointed upward, circling. "The one camera in this corner is new, added after the murder."

"Was this his customary parking spot?" Beau asked.

"Only senior management have assigned spaces, and those are on the upper level. For everyone else, it's a matter of grabbing what's available. Most of us tend to avoid this corner because it's dark and being so near the custodian's closet, there's always the possibility that you'll get dinged by one of their cleaning carts or something. Its only upside is that it's not far from the elevator."

"So, Mark probably parked in a different place every day," Beau mused. "Hard for someone to count on catching him here."

"Maybe not that hard," Carson added. "Most folks are creatures of habit and once they find an area they like, they'll generally go there. Many of our people take the very same spot all the time, unless a visitor or a new employee messes up their plan."

"So, this lot isn't for employees only?"

"There's a small visitor lot out front, in the open."

"Right. It's where we've parked every time."

"But there are others, say, vendors or contractors, people making deliveries. You probably noticed that we passed a security station near the upper elevator, on our way here. Employees scan their badges; others get a visitor pass. Same drill as if you enter through the front door."

"Okay. Good to know. Kind of rules out most outsiders."

"So, you're leaning toward the killer being an employee, then."

"Seems most likely. But, you know, I don't rule out anything."

Sam was staring at a dark stain on the concrete floor. "Is this?"

"Yeah, that's where it happened. Mark's car was in this slot and we guessed he was about to get into it."

She walked to the custodian's closet and tried the

doorknob. Locked. "Do you have a key?"

Carson unlocked the door, revealing a room about ten feet square. Shelves lined three walls, and four carts, similar to those used by hotel maids, stood in the open space. "The cleaning crew comes in the evenings, so all these carts are taken to other parts of the building."

"Mark was working late the night he died, I believe?"

Carson nodded.

"So. this closet might have been unlocked and someone could have waited in here, watching for him."

"I suppose so. I hadn't thought about it, but that makes sense. It was one of the cleaners who'd finished and was putting their stuff away who found him."

Beau thought about the scenario. If the killer was an employee, they'd have simply gone to their own vehicle and driven away, with no one the wiser. If it was someone else ... "Carson, if an outsider parked in this garage, they would have to go through the security gate before coming down here?"

"That's the protocol. Whether it's followed every single time, I really can't say."

"Does anyone track their movements, what times they come and go?"

"Again, that *should* be done. Is it done every time? I'm not sure."

So many tiny loopholes. Still, the number of people familiar with the procedures had to be fairly limited. Maybe this was something he could put Aiden onto, tracking down people who came and went that day, making sure everyone who came in also went out before nightfall.

They rode the elevator in silence, thanked the chief of security, and went back to their truck in the outdoor lot. As

Beau drove out toward the highway, Sam pulled something from the pocket of her jacket.

She laid out a wrinkled note on her lap, the paper edges curling like a dried leaf. The handwriting was a scrawl, barely legible. "Beau, I found this in the cleaning closet, half hidden under the edge of the shelving unit."

"Any idea what it is?" Beau leaned in, squinting, before directing his eyes back to the road.

Sam read the faint writing. "'The phoenix sings at dawn, where the silver stream meets the tarnished crown.' It's cryptic, but— We came across that name, the Phoenix Project. Wasn't there an emblem of a crown on that book? And silver, as in Sterling."

"Olivia Sterling?" Beau tried to reconcile the image of the straight-up businesswoman, her precise hair and clothing, with this poetic bit of verse. "We'd better get back to the paperwork on the Phoenix Project and see if we can make sense of this."

\* \* \*

Cecelia's kitchen had always been a sanctuary for her and Mark. The smell of fresh coffee filled the space, mingling with the late afternoon light that spilled across the tiled floor. She pictured him standing across the room, in conversation as they'd done so many times.

"Oh, honey, I wish you were here. Something's really off in Creston," Cecelia murmured, her fingers tracing the rim of her mug. "The rumors are flying and we just can't seem to come up with answers."

Mark, ever the pragmatist, folded his arms as he would have in real life, leaning back against the counter. "I told you I'd heard things. Rumors at work, whispers in the streets. And I was getting so close. Are you sure we want to pull at this thread, Cece?" he asked, his gaze not leaving hers.

"We have to," she insisted, her resolve steeling. "If we turn a blind eye, who will stand up for what's right? I can't let your killer go on living free, somewhere in this town. It scares me what they might do next."

Mark nodded slowly, agreeing. "All right. Dig deeper, but you and Beau watch your backs. If Olivia Sterling is involved …"

"Then we tread carefully," Cecelia finished, a fire kindling behind her eyes. "But we don't back down."

The vision faded abruptly when she heard the front door open. Beau appeared in the kitchen doorway.

"Did you receive a copy of Mark's autopsy report?"

She went blank for a moment. "What?"

"The Office of the Chief Medical Examiner. They perform autopsies here in the state, and immediate family can get a copy of the report."

Cece shook her head. "No, I haven't seen it."

"There's probably a form to fill out or a call to make. Let me find out."

"Beau, it's too hard. I can't—"

"You don't even have to read it if you don't want to. But I think there might be relevant information we never learned from the local police."

She nodded, dreading it but understanding.

# Chapter 28

Sam glanced at her watch while Cecelia made the call to the medical examiner's office to request the autopsy report. "Beau," she whispered, "I'm going to run by the library and see if I can catch Ethan before he closes up for the day."

He nodded absently, and she picked up the Toyota keys and headed out.

It was a little after five when she got there, and the sign said they closed at five-thirty. There was only one other car in the lot.

"Hey, Sam," Ethan greeted when she walked in. "How can I help you today?"

"I hate to say this, but it's come to our attention that there are some ugly rumors going around, allegations that Cecelia and Mark were up to some kind of shenanigans involving Sterling Microchips. That Mark was getting kickbacks or something, and Cece was in on it. It seems some of those stories may have originated with the book club that meets here."

Ethan sighed, his shoulders slumping. "I know, I've heard some of it."

"Well, can you squash it? We've found nothing in our investigation to show that Mark was doing anything wrong. In fact, he was looking into some shady doings by others within the company."

"Really? Like what?"

"I don't have a full enough picture yet to say. It would be speculation, and we know how speculation leads to untrue rumors being spread."

He nodded, his hands fiddling with a stack of cards.

"Anyway, I know the book club meets again tomorrow, so that's why I wanted to catch you now. Can you please say something—get them on some other track?"

"I'll do my best, Sam. I'm not really part of the club, you know. The library is just a meeting place for them." He squinted through his glasses and smiled.

She jammed her hands into her jacket pockets and nodded. "Thanks, I appreciate that, Ethan."

Down in her pocket, Sam felt the scrap of paper she'd found earlier. "Hey, one other question, if you have time."

"Sure, anything."

She read the words verbatim, then looked up. "Just wondering, do you know whether the references to a phoenix and a silver crown come from literature? It seems awfully poetic for something a cleaning person would be carrying around."

The librarian stood very still for a moment, then shrugged. "It's nothing I recognize. I'm pretty well versed in the classics, but this one doesn't ring a bell." He looked over at the paper. "Is that a handwritten note?"

"Yeah, but maybe it's something that fell out of a waste basket. I suppose one of the employees could have dreamed it up during their lunch hour."

He gave a light chuckle. "That's probably it exactly."

"Thanks again for anything you can do toward stopping those rumors about Cece. She'll appreciate it, I'm sure."

"Absolutely."

* * *

"I hope leftovers are okay for dinner," Cecelia said when Sam walked in. "I didn't have the energy to come up with anything else."

The scent of lasagna wafted from the oven, promising a repeat of the wonderful dinner from two nights ago. "I'd be happy to put together a salad," Sam offered. "Why don't you get a glass of wine and go put your feet up for fifteen minutes?"

Cece's look of gratitude was so profound Sam had to remind herself of all this poor woman had been through. Simple things, such as relaxing for a few minutes while someone else put dinner on the table, hadn't happened for a while now.

The salad came together in less than five minutes— chopping lettuce, cucumber, and tomato, and locating the bottle of Italian dressing. Sam walked into Mark's study, where she found Beau going through files.

"Want to take a break?" she asked.

"I will. Just flipping through this Phoenix Project book again, wondering if anything we've recently learned will add to our understanding of it."

"Find anything?"

"Not yet. But the night is young."

She stepped around the desk and went to the back of his chair so she could rub his neck and shoulders for him. "You're working awfully hard on this case."

"It's family. It's been an interesting case. And I want to get us back home in time for Thanksgiving."

"I thank you for that, and all my bakery customers thank you for that." The oven timer interrupted, and she dashed back to the kitchen to get the lasagna. "Dinner in five," she called out.

An hour later, properly stuffed with an excellent meal, Sam decided to get back to the Phoenix Project information while Beau watched a movie on TV with Cece. This time, she started at the end of the written pages, hoping to recreate a timeline from Cormorant's last days back to the beginning of whatever this Phoenix thing was.

There were references to contract negotiations, details about some equipment breakdowns that were suspected to be sabotage. That could be something vital, she thought, sticking a scrap of paper between pages to serve as a bookmark.

Three pages from the end, she ran into two solid pages neatly handwritten in what looked like Chinese characters. She studied them but, of course, had no clue what they said. Beau wouldn't know either, so there was no point in bothering him. She picked up the phone and called Aiden Wilder.

"I hope it's not too late to be talking business," she said.

He laughed. "Not at all. Now, if this had been last night,

I was out to dinner with a very nice young lady. Tonight, I'm home on my own, and what's on TV holds no interest."

"Okay, then, let me toss a strange question at you. Do you read Chinese?"

"Um, no. Not a bit. Why do you ask?"

"Remember the book of notes we found at the Cormorant factory, the one labeled Project Phoenix? I'm just now getting around to it and—"

"It's written in Chinese?"

"Not all of it, thank goodness, but a few pages are, yes."

She could practically hear his wheels turning as he digested this information.

"You know, cormorants are used as fishing birds in China—well, in many parts of Asia. So that's one possible connection. Maybe the company was named for those birds, and maybe the founder of Cormorant Industries comes from Chinese heritage."

"Whoever wrote these pages seems pretty proficient. And Olivia Sterling told us that Jay Cormorant, the head of the company, was Asian. So, maybe these are his notes."

"We might look for someone to translate them," he suggested. "Not that there are lots of people in Oklahoma fluent in Chinese, but I might locate someone through the university."

"Beau and I had talked about trying to locate Jay Cormorant, but we've been sidetracked by other things. Do you think you could find out where he went after the company shut down? I'm curious whether he stayed in this area."

"I'm getting on it right now," Aiden told her, the sound of a keyboard clicking in the background. "I'll give you a call when I learn something."

Sam was debating whether to go upstairs and handle the wooden box, in hopes it would enable her to translate another language, when Beau walked in.

"Movie over already?" she asked.

"I couldn't concentrate. Have you found anything new?" He gave a nod toward the book and she held up the pages of Chinese writing.

"Yes and no. But I talked to Aiden just now and he's trying to locate Jay Cormorant."

"Makes sense. We go to the source, rather than trying to decipher all this."

"Right. And we still might not know what it means."

"I'm tired. I'll be brushing my teeth." He squeezed her shoulder then walked out of the room.

Sam idly flipped through a few more pages. She felt tired too, not only from today's activities but the whole thing. She missed the bakery and her normal routine. Glancing at the time and knowing it was an hour earlier in New Mexico, she decided to give Kelly a call.

"I just got Ana to bed after two stories. She's reading them to me now." The sound of running water in the background made Sam think of the big kitchen in the warm and cozy Victorian back home. "So, what's up, Mom?"

"It feels like we're going in circles, frankly. We find interesting evidence and then it doesn't lead anywhere. I'm sure it will, eventually, but ..." She heard Cecelia moving around in the kitchen. "I'd rather hear about what's going on at home. Everything okay?"

"Pretty much the same old, same old. Jen said they had a big rush at Sweet's Sweets yesterday. Turns out Taos has a lot of November birthdays, I guess. But Julio and

Becky handled it great. Your financial bottom line should be looking good."

"And Riki? Has her mood improved?" Sam's phone chimed with an incoming call and she saw it was Aiden. "Oops. Do you mind if we take this up later? I should probably find out what this other call is about."

"No prob. I'm making a cup of chamomile and planning to read until bedtime. Later …!"

Sam tapped over to the other call. "Aiden, that was quick."

"Hey, I'm good. Or I just lucked out," he said with a laugh. "Jay Cormorant still lives in the area. Well, about a hundred miles away. I've got an address. You want me to go there and check him out?"

"Let me check with Beau. Maybe all three of us should go."

He read off the address, which was in Norman, a suburb on the south side of Oklahoma City. "Whatever works. Just let me know."

Sam found Beau in their bedroom, wearing soft pajama pants and a t-shirt. She filled him in on Aiden's find and the PI's offer to pay a visit to Jay Cormorant.

"I'm guessing by the sparkle in your eyes, you'd be up for a short road trip tomorrow." He grinned at her. "I know. I'm feeling kind of unsettled here, too."

She walked over to the window and closed the drapes against the darkness outside. "Maybe three of us popping in on this guy would be a bit much. I should let Aiden know that you and I can handle it."

"Good. I'd like a day of having you to myself anyhow."

So, that became the plan. Sam went back downstairs to the study to gather the papers she would need for the next day, put the rest in Mark's safe, and say goodnight to Cece.

By nine the next morning they were on the road.

* * *

Beau's GPS guided them to a modest home in an older neighborhood of similar clapboard-sided houses. This one was painted pale green. Inside Sam's backpack in the back seat was the wooden box, and she gave it a gentle caress before getting out of the truck.

They walked through a short chain-link gate and up a cracked sidewalk, then tapped at the screen door. A female voice shouted something unintelligible and a minute later a man opened the door. Sam noted that he was Asian, probably in his eighties, and somewhat stooped in the shoulders. His gray hair could use a trim, and he stared out, assessing the strangers at his door.

"Are you Jay Cormorant?" Beau asked.

A nod.

"We're up in Creston, looking into the death of a relative. He used to work for Sterling Microchips, and we understand you once had a connection with that company. May we come in and ask you a couple of questions?"

Cormorant tilted his head, considering, then pushed the screen door open and stepped aside. As they walked into a small living room, the man turned and rattled off a series of rapid-fire instructions. Sam assumed the language was Mandarin. A young woman bustled into the room, straightening a few items on a coffee table, then grabbing a jacket, a blanket, and two pairs of shoes and swooshing back out.

"Sorry for the informality of our home." he said with

a flawless American accent. "Please. Sit." He indicated two chairs and he took the sofa, which sagged noticeably when he sat. Other pieces in the room carried Asian themes, from the lacquered screen in one corner to the collection of cloisonne vases in a beautiful, glossy black display cabinet.

The young woman appeared at the doorway again and a few words were exchanged. She bowed from the waist and backed out.

"Your home is lovely, Mr. Cormorant," Sam said. "Do the art pieces come from China?"

"Ah, yes. I, myself, came from China. My birth name was Chen Ji, but I was very young when my family came here, and my parents Americanized our names, so I was known as Jay Chen, for the lucky bird in my horoscope. When I went into business, my auspicious sign was the cormorant, a wonderful bird and helpful to those who earn their living by fishing." He gave a small laugh. "My business was not related to fishing, but I loved those birds. I changed my name to Jay Cormorant, in honor of my two lucky signs."

Sam nodded. "I like that."

The young woman appeared again, bearing a tray with a teapot and three small cups, which she set on the table in front of the man.

"My daughter, Jennifer Chen," he said.

"Sorry I can't join you," she said, her earlier formality gone. "I have to get ready for work."

"Manager of a restaurant, a very popular one," he told them once she had left the room. "She's saving to buy the place."

He poured tea and handed out the cups. "Now. You mentioned Sterling Microchips. You're going back in history, young man," Cormorant said. "I don't know what I can tell you."

Beau gave a quick recap of how he'd been called in to look into the death of his cousin's husband, the fact that the trail in Mark's files had led them to Cormorant Industries, and that they'd learned there had been a negotiation of some kind between Cormorant and Sterling Enterprises.

"We went out to your old location and were amazed to find a lot of equipment and some of the paperwork still in the building."

"I'm surprised. We had suffered some financial setbacks. I assumed the bank had claimed our possessions and sold them to pay the loans."

Sam shook her head. "Apparently they didn't."

"We spoke with Olivia Sterling and she said there was talk of partnering your two companies. What happened to that?"

The old man sat back against the cushions. "I discovered things. About that business. Things I did not want to become involved with, no matter how much I could have used the money."

"What types of things?"

Cormorant paused and Beau gave him a long moment to consider.

"I felt they were using me. No, that is not right. It was not a feeling. It was a fact. I learned that the Sterling people wanted a relationship with me because of my family ties in China."

"I see. Many American companies have connections in China. It's how business is done these days, isn't it?"

"I have two brothers who went back to China in our adult years. Established very successful businesses, became very wealthy. Of course, the Chinese government watches them carefully, takes a large portion. It's a form of control."

"And Sterling wanted to work with you, in order to gain access to your brothers and their businesses?"

He nodded. "In the end, it did not matter. They found ways in, I guess you would say, through the back door. They made the connections they needed, without my help. And I am glad of that. I did not want to be involved."

Sam reached into her pocket and pulled out the scrap of paper she'd found in the maintenance supply room at Sterling. She read aloud from the faint writing. "'The phoenix sings at dawn, where the silver stream meets the tarnished crown.' Do you know what that means?"

Cormorant shook his head. "Sorry, it doesn't seem familiar."

Sam spoke up. "What's Project Phoenix?"

"Nothing, now. At the time, it was the name we assigned to the potential partnership. How do you know about this?"

"Among the papers left behind at your factory were references to it."

"Ah. I can see I should have personally supervised the clearing of the building."

"Once we've finalized our case, we can return the papers we removed."

Cormorant shook his head. "I am, as they say, over it. The business was my livelihood for some years, but I do not wish to go back."

"Can you tell me about your conversations with Mark Mitchell?"

"This was your cousin who died?" The weathered face became sad. "He was a good man, maybe too good, wanting to see crimes punished."

"Crimes … specifically?"

"He told me he was an accountant within the Sterling organization and he had uncovered theft and embezzlement. He needed more information in order to go to the police."

"Did you have the information he needed?"

A shrug. "I don't know. I also had seen things that did not sit well with me. When he showed me a shipping label addressed to my brothers' businesses in Shanghai, I knew what was happening. Sterling did not need me. They had found a way to reach my brothers. I believed the fact that I refused to participate in their 'off the books' sales, that is why they backed out of our deal."

Sam wasn't sure how to ask her next question. "We found something in Mark's papers that makes it look like … maybe he gave you some money?"

"Like a bribe? No. Nothing like that. Did his record show that I returned the money, never cashed his check?"

She shook her head.

"Mark wanted to give me money for the information I provided, but I refused. He visited me here, in my home, saw that our circumstances are not exactly, shall we say, elegant. When he sent the check, he said he only wanted to help us out. I did not want any help that tied me to those people, that Jason Blackwood. I do not like that man."

"Do you think Blackwood was responsible for Mark's death?" Beau asked.

"It would not surprise me."

And there they had it, another witness who believed Blackwood was behind the murder.

# Chapter 29

Sam was fairly quiet on the ride back to Creston. She'd sensed no deception from Jay Cormorant, was actually pleased he had been so forthcoming.

"Now we just need to figure out whether Blackwood was the one wielding the knife that night in the garage, or if he used some type of hired muscle." Beau seemed to be reading her thoughts.

It was late afternoon when they arrived back at Cecelia's, after having lunch at the restaurant where Cormorant's daughter worked. There were less obvious ways to help out someone who could use a little extra money, they'd decided, leaving a substantial tip.

The mail had arrived, and Cece was standing in the front hall, staring at an envelope. "I can't open it," she said, handing it to Beau.

Office of the Chief Medical Examiner. The words leapt out from the return address.

"Shall I open it in the other room?" he asked.

She nodded, her eyes welling up. Sam waited with Cece, without a clue what to say or do.

"I'm going to make a cup of hot chocolate, Sam. You don't need to babysit me. I've had many moments like this in recent months, and I always get through them."

Sam thought of offering to make the cocoa herself, but realized that Cece probably just wanted a few minutes alone and a task to occupy her mind. She made her way up to their bedroom where Beau had gone.

He handed her the two sheets of paper. One was a standard form containing the basic facts: name, address, and such, along with some generic outlines of a human shape, front and back. Hand-drawn elements showed the locations and positioning of the wounds. The conclusion page seemed pretty basic: Subject cause of death was a stab wound to the aorta. Contributing wounds severed pulmonary arteries. Depth of wounds indicate a six-inch blade.

"Is this anything we didn't already know?" Sam handed the pages back to him.

"Actually, it's significant. Did you notice that all the wounds were on the front of the body."

"And …"

"None from behind. Sam, what it means is that it's likely Mark knew his killer. You have to get in close to inflict stab wounds. A stranger would have a hard time walking right up, within an arm's length, without a fight. There are no defensive wounds on Mark's arms, no misdirected 'slices' where the knife glanced off. Three direct punctures."

"Oh, God."

"And, if you'll recall from the scene at the garage, the blood stain was where the rear of the vehicle would have been. Presumably, late at night there wouldn't have been lots of cars parked there, so plenty of space for Mark to make a run for it."

"And if a stranger had approached him, with a knife in hand, Mark would have surely tried to escape or at least defend himself in some way."

"Which tells me he probably knew this person, waited, standing there as they approached him."

Sam swallowed hard. "I can see why Cece didn't want to read this. Knowing the details makes it worse. We're not telling her, are we?"

"Not unless she asks, and even then, I'd give only the basics. Yeah, I think it's too much for her right now."

\* \* \*

They found Cece in the living room, staring out the front windows with her empty mug on her lap.

"I'm thinking barbeque would taste real good tonight," Beau said. "Can I treat you ladies to a night out?"

Cece shook her head. "I don't want to see people right now."

"Understood. Then how about if I go and pick up some sandwiches?" That suggestion was met with a smile.

He walked out to his truck and realized he didn't have a particular destination in mind. Rather than bother Cece with another detail, he would drive around until he found something that looked good. Four blocks from the house he realized he was being tailed by a white police car with blue markings.

"Okay, buddy, I'm not doing anything wrong," he muttered, eyeing his speedometer.

He pulled to a full stop at the next intersection, minded all the rules, and made a righthand turn. The cruiser did the same. Ahead, he spotted Bubba's Bar-B-Q. This was the same fellow who'd cooked the fabulous ribs at the picnic the other day. The perfect answer to what his tastebuds wanted. He signaled and pulled in. The patrol car went on past.

Beau came out ten minutes later with a box laden with baby-back ribs, glazed chicken breasts, pulled pork, slider rolls, coleslaw, and potato salad—enough to feed the household for days. He knew Sam would tease him, but he just wanted to cover all the bases, in case Cecelia didn't feel like getting out right away. Whatever they didn't eat could go into the freezer.

Two blocks from Bubba's, another Creston police vehicle slid in behind him. This was an SUV, dark blue with white markings.

"Seriously?" Beau made a quick left turn and the car followed. A right turn onto a residential street, same result. "Okay, man. You know who I am and you know where I'll be going. So, what's with the tail?"

He knew the answer to that. Rollie Benson was being a jerk. It was harassment of the most basic kind, the type where he'd be cited for a broken taillight or some other little thing. He circled back to the main drag through town, taking his time, obeying every law. When he entered Cece's development, the SUV peeled away.

He was still a little wound up over the whole incident when he walked into the kitchen with his box of goodies.

"Oh my, that smells incredible, Beau!" The smile on

his cousin's face made the trip worth it.

"Dig in," he told them. "I couldn't decide what everyone would want, so I almost got some of everything."

Sam laughed. "This looks more like Thanksgiving dinner than what I'd make at home."

"Minus the pies. I'm counting on those, you know."

They loaded plates and decided to sit at the breakfast room table instead of the counter this time. As soon as they'd made some inroads into the food supply, he brought up the subject of the police tail.

"These were Creston PD vehicles, so I assume Rollie Benson is the one who's ordered them to watch us."

"Does that mean we're getting close to learning who the killer is?" Sam paused with a forkful of potato salad in midair.

"If it is, they're a lot more confident in our findings than I am. I'm still not convinced Jason Blackwood is the knife-wielding type, but I don't know who is." He glanced across the table. "I'm sorry, Cece, I didn't mean to bring this up."

"I understand. It's okay."

"I'm just mentioning it so you two will be careful when you go out. I don't want you to take any chances, trying to outrun them or anything dumb like that. But keep in mind our movements are probably being reported to Benson. Try to keep your errands benign looking so they don't have any reason to pull you in and question you."

"You think they would do that?" Sam asked.

"I don't know, but we must be getting close to something. This is the first time one of them has been right behind me." The first one I've seen, he thought. How long had Benson and his officers actually been following their movements?

"This is creeping me out," Cece said. "Do you think they've got the house bugged or can listen in on our phone calls?"

Beau pictured the simple police station. Very low tech, very small town. "I doubt it. The security detail out at Sterling is better equipped than the police department here."

"Could Sterling be behind it?" Sam asked, her eyes sharp.

"Doubtful. For one thing, Carson would let me know if he'd received those types of orders. Rollie Benson may have some ulterior reason for why his department never investigated this crime, but I don't get the feeling the town and the chip factory are completely in cahoots with each other."

Sam had a troubled look on her face, and Beau reached over and squeezed her hand. "Just be aware. That's all I'm saying."

* * *

Sam couldn't get the dinner conversation out of her mind. Coupled with their trip to meet Jay Cormorant this morning, her thoughts were swirling and no amount of deep breathing was helping her to fall asleep. When Beau began snoring softly beside her, she got out of bed, slipped into sweats, and walked down to Mark's study.

The Project Phoenix book and papers lay on the desk, but she felt Jay had covered that subject already. He seemed convinced that Jason Blackwood was behind Mark's death, so it seemed unlikely anything in the book would contradict that. But something else Jay had told them kept nagging at her.

Maybe there were details about the embezzling and theft he'd alluded to, and she began to feel a certainty that the answer was in something they'd left behind at the old Cormorant Industries warehouse. If she could come up with some positive proof against Jason, they could turn it over to state or federal authorities. Someone higher up than the Creston PD, for sure.

She walked through the darkened house, navigating by the small nightlights Cecelia left in each room, standing at the tall living room windows and staring out at the moonlit yard. A stiff breeze whipped the tree branches, then died down. The answers were out there.

"And I just want to find them quickly so we can go home," she whispered to the night.

# Chapter 30

The garage door slid silently closed and the Toyota SUV rolled out of the driveway. What am I doing? Sam asked herself. And then she answered: Taking advantage of a quiet time when no one will catch me at what I'm about to do.

She patted her backpack on the passenger seat beside her, belatedly wondering whether she should have brought her carved wooden box with her. When she'd grabbed her pack, she'd pulled the box out to hold it until the wood warmed to her touch. But she wanted to travel light for this mission, so she'd left it sitting on the hall table. If all went according to plan, she'd be back in under an hour.

Leaving Cece's development, Sam saw no other vehicles on the road, and a quick ten minutes later she spotted the abandoned Cormorant Industries building at the side of the highway. She pulled off the road, circling to the back of the building and tucking her vehicle into the shadows. Reaching into her pack she grabbed her lockpicks and flashlight, then stuffed her phone and wallet into the deep pockets of her jacket. The breeze had quickened and she zipped her jacket against the chill.

It was a little awkward to aim the beam of her light at the lock, while using two hands to operate the tools, but this was a remembered skill from her years of entering abandoned houses. Her fingers took over and the lock yielded to her touch. In under a minute she was inside, sweeping her light across the huge space. The old equipment stood sentinel, making her think of Jay Cormorant and the days when this would have been a bustling business. She began to move, keeping the flashlight beam aimed toward the floor to avoid tripping.

A skittery sound came from behind the silent equipment, probably mice. She hoped there weren't rats. A low, windy howl came through a broken place in one window. Sam shivered at the sound, then took a deep breath as she made her way to the basement stairs and descended. The safe sat there, as before, and she remembered the digits of the combination from their last visit. She walked to it, entered the numbers, and the door swung open. She propped her light against a brick she found in one corner, illuminating the safe's interior.

Outside, it sounded like the wind was picking up, perhaps becoming a full-fledged storm. "Don't get sidetracked," she admonished herself. Her own voice echoed back from the safe's hard metal surfaces.

On their prior visit she had concentrated on taking the Phoenix Project book and related files, but now she felt she had Jay Cormorant's implicit permission to look further. She pulled two small drawers open, but they were empty. On a narrow shelf she found what she was looking for, a file labeled Sterling Enterprises.

She recognized Mark's handwriting on the label. A quick peek inside showed what she'd come here for, handwritten notes he must have prepared for his meeting with Jay Cormorant. There was no time to read through it. That could be done back at the house. She pushed the safe door closed without locking it, then picked up her flashlight.

A chill breeze flowed down the stairs, the wind picking up dramatically in the last few minutes. She made her way up, closed the door to the basement, and started across the factory floor toward the exit.

Something whacked her arm, sending the flashlight flying, and then the world went dark.

# Chapter 31

Beau's phone erupted with an insistent buzz, shattering the silence of the bedroom. He came out of a deep sleep. Sam wasn't in the bed beside him.

The screen flashed *unknown*, yet he knew better than to ignore it; his gut twisted into a tight coil. He swiped at the screen, and the voice that crackled through chilled his blood.

"Listen close, *Sheriff*," the distorted voice sneered. "Your lady's got something to say."

In the background, a sound scraped—metal against concrete.

"Go ahead, talk to him," coached the angry voice. Long seconds of silence. "Now!"

"Beau—Cormorant!"

The sharp sound of a slap came through.

"Sam!" Every muscle in his body coiled like a spring. Anger surged through him as he paced the bedroom, red-hot and fierce, drowning out the taunting laughter on the other end.

"We got your attention now?" The kidnapper's voice oozed confidence.

"Let. Her. Go." Beau's voice went cold but his mind raced with fragmented thoughts. He needed a plan, fast. The image of Samantha—scared, alone, depending on him—seared into his brain, fueling his resolve.

"Tick tock, Beau," the voice drawled before the line went dead.

The phone slipped from Beau's grasp, thumping onto the nightstand. He stood motionless for a heartbeat, feeling the thrum of his pulse in his ears. This was serious, deadly serious. Adrenaline replaced shock, propelling him into action. Samantha needed him, and he'd move heaven and earth to bring her home.

He pulled jeans on, grabbed his pistol from where he'd stashed it under the mattress, and raced through the huge house, hitting light switches, scanning every window and door, for a sign of how the kidnappers had entered.

Both front and back doors were secure. He heard a sound behind him and spun toward it, pistol raised.

"Beau?" Cecelia squinted at the lights, her face sleepy. "What's going on?"

"Sam's been kidnapped!" He knew his face must look wild; he saw it in the way Cece looked at him.

"Ohmygosh, Beau. Wha—"

He forced himself to stand completely still for a moment and breathe. His frantic-husband side wanted to lash out, to run, to shoot someone. But his law-enforcement side told him that would be stupid. He needed to think, to be clear-headed as he assembled the facts.

"Go around and check every window," he told his cousin. He'd already given most of them a cursory glance, but this would keep her busy and out of his way for a few minutes.

Something near the front door had caught his attention and he went there now. Sam's backpack purse was missing. The wooden box, which she'd carried with her when they went to visit Jay Cormorant, sat on the hall table. He placed his hands on top of it, the way he'd seen her do. It was cool to the touch.

With deliberate steps, he walked through the kitchen and approached the connecting door to the garage. The Toyota was gone.

Cece joined him in the kitchen. "All the windows are fine."

Then he remembered Sam's frantic voice over the phone. She had shouted one word: Cormorant. Had she gone out there on her own? Why?

He cursed under his breath. Was he going to have to kill that hardheaded woman?

# Chapter 32

Sam cursed herself for her stupidity. Why had she come out here on her own, and why hadn't she at least left Beau a note. Because she'd fully believed she would grab the proof they needed from the safe and she would be right back. And it had almost gone that way.

Now she had to assess her situation and figure out how to get out of it. Her hands and feet were bound; a black bag of some scratchy material covered her head. She ran a fingertip toward her wrist, feeling the smooth fabric of her jacket. At least she seemed to be fully clothed.

She took a mental inventory of what she'd had with her, providing the kidnappers hadn't searched her pockets and emptied them. She had come with a flashlight, lockpicks, her wallet and keys. What else? The flashlight was most certainly gone; her last conscious thought had been when it flew out of her hand as she left the basement. She stretched and patted her pockets, but none of the other items seemed good candidates for warding off her attackers.

Cormorant. She was fairly certain she'd shouted the word out to Beau when the bad guys called and taunted him. Would he know that's where she went? Would he come alone? Please, no, she prayed. He would need time to gather some help. Who would he bring?

Don't call the police. She concentrated the thought toward Beau. Surely he wouldn't trust Benson or any of his men. Right now, more than anything, she didn't want Beau and Cece walking into the same trap.

A door slammed, echoing through a hollow space. She tried to envision her surroundings. Maybe she was in the main part of the factory, and the men were searching the building for others she might have brought with her. She honed her senses to pay attention to voices and footsteps, trying to calculate how many were here.

If she could free herself from the bonds that held her, she might be able to overpower one guy. Or she might be able to sneak away from two. But at the moment she had a sick feeling there were at least three of them.

Her wrists were bound with rope—she figured that out by the feel of it as she tried to pick at the knots. It was fairly hopeless; the angle was too awkward. A tiny sound sent all her senses to full alert.

"Don't bother." The whispered voice was close enough she could smell stale breath.

A vise-like grip took hold of her left ankle and she sensed sawing action on the ropes there. "Hold still, you stupid cow."

She did. The sawing continued. The moment she felt the rope give way, she kicked out. But the man was quicker. "Dumb b—"

"She's a feisty one," said another voice, also male. "Come on, get her up."

Sam tried to plant all her weight on the seat of the chair, but strong hands took hold of her arms and forced her forward. For one silly second, she thought of going limp, falling to the floor, and making them try to pick her up. Her unwanted thirty pounds might become her ally. But then she realized they would begin kicking, and they could do a lot more damage if she were prone on the ground.

A hand shoved her from the back and others gripped her arms, forcing her to walk alongside them. When she felt the chill breeze through the fabric over her face, she knew this was not good. She dragged her feet, but they maneuvered her into the backseat of a vehicle.

# Chapter 33

Beau didn't apologize for calling Aiden in the middle of the night. The private investigator seemed instantly alert, aware there was a problem.

"Sam's been kidnapped. I got a call."

"Demands?"

"No. They just wanted to taunt me with the fact they have her."

"Okay, let's break it down. What clues did you get from the call?"

"She shouted 'Cormorant' before they cut her off."

"So, you think she was back at that abandoned factory?"

"Could be. Probably. The whole call was maybe ten seconds, but it sounded close, indoors, echoey. I don't think it was an outdoor space."

Aiden went quiet for a minute and Beau could picture

him pacing. "Okay, I'll call my contact in the state highway patrol, the guy I'd already talked to about the previous kidnappings. He'll take me seriously."

"I'm heading out to Cormorant's warehouse now." Beau was already pulling on more clothes and checking his pistol.

"Not by yourself, Beau. Wait for me, at least."

"Meet me there. I need to assess the situation and come up with a plan to get her back."

"Right. But don't go in alone."

Beau wanted to resist the advice, but wasn't this exactly what he was feeling so angry about, the fact Sam had gone there alone?

He told Cecelia to stay home, to keep her phone nearby, and to let him know if she heard anything at all. Zipping his warm coat, he ran out to his truck and whipped out of the driveway. The drive to the old warehouse had never felt so long.

He cut his headlights and rolled onto the property slowly. The building was dark, not a sliver of light from any of the windows or around the doors. When he circled to the back, he saw Sam's Toyota near the walk-in door. No other vehicles. He stopped his truck a short distance away, at what would have been the far corner of the parking lot in the old days. About a minute later, Aiden drove in and stopped beside him.

They spoke through their open windows. "No sign of anyone," Beau said, holding up the binoculars he'd used. "From here it looks like the door might be open a crack."

"Highway patrol have dispatched two units from their Enid office. They should be along any time."

"It's too quiet. I don't like this." Beau got out of his truck, pocketing the key.

"Agreed." Aiden left his SUV in place and the two walked cautiously toward the building.

Beau placed a hand on the hood of the Toyota Sam had driven here. No warmth there. Aiden gave a nod toward the walk-in door and gestured for them to approach on both sides of it. Beau's recon had been correct. The door stood open a couple of inches. He nudged it with the toe of his boot and it swung inward. Both men switched on flashlights.

Keeping the lights aimed at the floor, they edged inside. Wind whistled above, through some of the broken windows. A dozen feet in to their right, fresh scrape marks marred the concrete floor. They led to a chair that had tipped over. Two short lengths of rope lay a few feet away. Scuffed footprints in the dust led toward the door through which they'd just entered.

"Looks like they've come and gone," Aiden whispered.

Beau shone his light farther into the room, toward the glassed-in offices on the left, which they'd previously explored. That must have been where the chair came from. He spotted the door to the basement, which stood open, and a scattering of papers on the floor nearby.

He listened, wary of a trap, but the place echoed with each footstep he took and he heard nothing else. He stooped and picked up a manila folder. Sterling Enterprises, said the label. It was in Mark's handwriting. Sam had been onto something after all.

"Beau!" Aiden stage-whispered, pointing toward the door.

The soft crunch of gravel alerted them and they each ducked behind nearby equipment. The vehicle rolled to a stop and a door quietly opened.

"Oklahoma Highway Patrol! Come out with your hands up!"

Aiden relaxed. "Come on, our reinforcements are here."

"It's Aiden Wilder," he shouted back. "I'm here with the sheriff of Taos County. We're coming out."

It took a couple minutes for them to reassure the other four men and identify themselves. Beau gave a quick recap of the situation. "This is the vehicle my wife was driving. Inside, we haven't found a sign of anyone but it would be smart to double check. Odds are they've already left in whatever vehicles they came in."

The state troopers took him seriously and fanned out with bright lights and pistols drawn.

# Chapter 34

Sam tried to pay attention for signs that would tell her where they were going, but it was impossible. Her equilibrium was off; with her face covered and hands bound, it was all she could do to ride along and not become nauseated. She determined there were three men, one driving, one in the shotgun seat, and the other beside her, on her right. The car was most likely a high-end sedan of some kind; it had a cushy suspension and she recalled being told to duck her head as they pushed her inside. They'd belted her into the middle seat of the back, so no way to reach for the door handle and attempt an escape.

There a number of turns, but few stops. She guessed they didn't want to risk driving through a city with a hooded passenger in the back. The thought almost made her chuckle. Almost.

She'd briefly held the carved box before she left Cece's house, and now she tried to call upon any residual power to help her out of this situation, but it felt futile. She hadn't been able to overpower any of the men or to magically undo the knots in her ropes.

The one thing she had going for her was that her feet were now free. They would need her to walk when they got to their destination. She began to formulate a plan for what to do when she got out of the car. Smack one of them? Get the hood off her head if she could? Run!

She just wished she knew whether they had guns. The surprise attack had left her woefully short on knowledge about her captors.

# Chapter 35

Beau gathered the papers that must have fallen from the folder. They were the one piece of evidence he possessed now, and probably the last things Sam had touched. He felt a catch in his throat and the questions flooded in. If he'd never come here to investigate Mark's murder, if he'd never encouraged Sam to help with his investigations. He should have left her alone to bake her beautiful pastries and stay out of ugly situations like this one.

"Beau?" Aiden appeared at his side.

Beau cleared his throat and blinked hard to hide the moisture in his eyes.

"The officers would like to talk with us, to see if we have any other ideas."

"Sure." He saw the four state troopers gathered near

the door. They stepped outside together, one of the officers locking the door behind them.

The senior of the four men spoke up. "We'd all be more comfortable out of this wind, if you would like to come with us to the station and help us fill in the blanks. I can probably guarantee we'll come up with some fresh coffee."

Beau nodded. He knew the drill. And although he'd much rather be alone with his thoughts right now, to be able to piece together the puzzle, common sense told him he wasn't going to solve this alone. Having input from the others would be beneficial, and having the authority of the state police would be crucial.

He and Aiden climbed into their own vehicles and followed the two black-and-whites into Enid. During the ride, he phoned Cecelia, mainly to reassure her that he was okay, hoping she might have received some word directly from Sam. No such luck.

The next three hours slid by in a blur. There was coffee, and somewhere about the time dawn was beginning to show through the windows, someone brought in some breakfast sandwiches. Beau and Aiden shared what they knew about the previous kidnappings, learning belatedly that the state police had largely been kept in the dark about that. Their chief promised to have a serious talk with Rollie Benson. From his tone, Beau thought an inquiry could begin proceedings for the firing of Creston's local rube.

Fitting, he thought. Someone needed to clean up that little town.

Beau felt talked-out and exhausted in that crazy way that also included being way too wired for sleep—something like jetlag. He drove back to Creston in a mental fog, thinking he wanted time alone. The idea of going directly back to Cece's and having to repeat the whole story one more time was just too much.

Instead, he steered toward the town center, finding himself outside the town hall and police station. It was still early. None of the government employees would be here yet; only a dim set of nightlights glowed from inside the large building. Across the square, the café was open, but he didn't need food, coffee, or company. He parked in front of the closed hardware store and got out of his truck. Maybe a brisk walk would do the trick.

Hands in pockets, he navigated the sidewalk until he came to the corner. From the narrow alley beside him came the dim glow from a streetlamp as it flickered out. He realized he wasn't alone. A silhouette materialized from the early morning shadows—a poised figure with unmistakable confidence.

"Olivia?" Beau's voice cut through the silence, sharp with suspicion. He squinted at her form, the tight bun and power posture unmistakably hers. "What are you doing here?"

"Beau." Olivia's tone was even, her heels a soft click on the stone. "I'm glad I found you. I heard about Sam; I'm here to help."

His brow furrowed. "How?" Trust didn't come easy these days. But there she stood, out of place yet strangely at ease among the trash bins and graffiti walls.

"Carson Delaney. He's related to the Enid Chief of Police. They talked this morning."

He still wasn't clear on why Olivia wanted to get involved but if she had information that could crack the case wide open, he was here to listen.

"Talk," he said, his voice terse.

She glanced over her shoulder before leaning in, her voice a conspiratorial whisper. "I've been investigating too—the same questions Mark raised."

A surge of adrenaline shot through Beau. "Olivia Sterling, CEO by day, sleuth by night? I have to say, that's an unexpected twist."

She gave a dry, humorless laugh but her expression was urgent, her tone sincere.

Beau's instincts told him to be wary, but something held him in place. She glanced down the alleyway once more before she spoke again, her voice low.

"Jason's behind it all," she started, "he's been using my company as a front for his dirty work. I ignored the signs at first, but when things started to not add up, when others reported that the shipping numbers were off … I dug deeper."

"Wait, does this pertain to Sam getting kidnapped?" Beau interrupted, his thoughts racing. The pieces didn't want to fit together, not yet.

"I believe so. In fact, I think it's what was behind all the disappearances and my people leaving their jobs so quickly," she confirmed with a nod. Her hands, usually so steady and commanding at the office, now betrayed a faint tremor. "He's orchestrated everything—the smuggling, the theft. It's all happening under our noses."

"Under your nose, you mean." Beau's tone was sharp, but his gaze was fixed on Olivia's face, searching for the truth.

Olivia met his stare unflinchingly. "I've been collecting evidence. Emails, transactions, inventory discrepancies. I can prove it."

"Show me."

She reached into her coat, retrieving a flash drive. "Everything is here. The numbers don't lie, Beau. We've been shipping out more chips than we've been producing."

Beau turned the flash drive over in his hand, its weight insignificant compared to the gravity of what it represented. His mind vibrated with the revelation. Olivia Sterling, not just a CEO, but an undercover agent against her own executives.

"Mark Mitchell knew. He gave me this flash drive and I checked it out," Olivia added. "He caught on to the shipments, started asking questions. That's why he's gone, Beau."

"Damn it." The words left his lips as a whisper. Beau thought back to Mark—quiet, observant, probably too clever for his own good.

"Be careful with this information," Olivia warned. "Jason's reach goes far. And not everyone who seems trustworthy is on our side."

"Understood." Beau pocketed the flash drive, his mind already ticking through the next steps. He looked at the CEO, her blonde hair still perfectly in place, her eyes fierce with determination. She was a powerhouse, but could he trust her?

"I get it. You have every right to be wary," she said, noticing his expression. "But I had to play my cards close to the chest. It was the only way to collect what we needed without tipping them off."

"Who is 'them'?" he asked, watching Olivia carefully.

"Local law enforcement," Olivia replied, her eyes darting left and right. "Creston cops are bought and paid for, every last one of them."

Her statement confirmed what he'd already suspected.

"Which means," Olivia continued, lowering her voice, "we can't take this to them. We'll need the highway patrol and the feds to step in if we want any arrests made. But our evidence must be ironclad."

"Got it. I've got contacts there already."

"Be smart about who you talk to. Jason Blackwood doesn't go for trivial games—he plays for keeps."

"Understood," Beau said, his expression grim.

"Good luck."

"Thanks, Olivia," he said finally, a hint of respect coloring his tone.

"I'm putting my money behind taking down this theft ring, Beau. And I want us to get Sam back, alive and well." She turned, ready to leave.

"Thank you."

# Chapter 36

Beau pocketed the flash drive and walked back to his truck. When he arrived at Cecelia's house, the place was dark. He quietly let himself in. A faint trace of coffee scent drifted on the air, but the kitchen was abandoned. She must have gone back to bed after his call a while ago.

He made his way to Mark's study, closed the door, and turned on a lamp before booting up the laptop and inserting the flash drive. A spreadsheet was the only file. He opened it.

"Wish you were here right now, Sam," he muttered. Then he caught himself. Of course he did. If she were here, he wouldn't be digging into this. Then again, would he have simply taken Olivia's word that this was the proof they needed to go after Jason Blackwood?

He forced his exhausted mind to focus. What he needed,

at this moment, were names of Jason's accomplices. He couldn't envision Jason lurking about in the abandoned Cormorant factory, catching Sam, and taking her somewhere. He would have thugs for that because men like Jason always created layers between themselves and their crimes.

Mark had detailed his findings and created a sort of hierarchy of names. Beau pulled out a notepad and jotted down several of them. Then he dialed Aiden.

"I'll apologize in advance if I woke you. I know it was a long night."

The young investigator gave a gruff laugh. "No sleep for the weary right now. There's too much to do. What's up?"

Beau quickly described his encounter with Olivia Sterling and the contents of the flash drive. "I've got three names, men listed as cohorts of Jason's. Can you check them out? Let me know if they're Sterling employees, and get addresses and any other detail—no matter how small—that might tell us if they are the ones who took Sam and where they might be holding her."

"Glad to. I'm on it."

"I'll call Carson Delaney and ask what he may know about them, and see if he'd be willing to have his security detail search the building from top to bottom."

"You think they'd dare take her to Olivia's property?"

"I know, it's farfetched and I'm grasping at straws here."

"No, no. Good to check out every possibility."

Beau read the names from his list, to get Aiden started, then he called Carson.

"Sorry it's early, man, but there's been a bad development overnight."

"I'm aware. How can I help? Anything at all."

"First of all, do you know if any of these men are Sterling employees?" He gave the same names he'd shared with Aiden.

"Well, yes, all of them. Hal Emerson and Ronnie Glasser are the two who usually work the guard shack at the entrance gate. Joe Sparling moonlights parttime here in maintenance, but you may have met him already as part of the Creston PD."

Beau vaguely remembered his first visit to that department but didn't recall any of the officers' names, other than Chief Benson.

Carson was still talking. "You may recall that I said Jason Blackwood directly hired and supervised the guards at the gate? That's making a lot more sense to me now."

Beau was thinking the very same thing. And he would bet money that either Emerson or Glasser had planted the tracking device on his truck that first day. They knew, from his visit to the police department, exactly who he was and why he was in town.

"Aiden is tracking down their home addresses, but I need to know … Can you think of anywhere these guys may have taken Sam? Is there any chance they brought her there, to the Sterling building?"

"I doubt that, just because of the risk to them, but I'll conduct a quiet search. She won't be in any of the offices or hallways, nowhere visible. So, it'll be a closet or storage place, maybe the mechanical spaces in the building."

"The sooner the better," Beau said. "They've held her for several hours already. And remember, Olivia Sterling offered her help. Call on her if you need to."

"I'll get back to you the minute I know something."

When Beau's phone rang less than two minutes later, he nearly laughed. "Well, that was quick."

But it was Aiden. "I went ahead and had the state PD dispatch units to the home addresses of all three men, but I learned something else that might be a lead. Joe Sparling's brother-in-law owns the bowling alley on 18th Street. It's only open in the evenings. It'd be the perfect place to stash someone out of the way."

"Let's go."

"It's going to take more than the two of us to search a building of that size."

"Carson and his team are going through the Sterling Enterprises facility, floor by floor. They'll be tied up for a while. Can we get more police units?"

"Let me try the county sheriff. He owes me a favor. And I'll request that the staties join us once they've eliminated all of the suspects' homes."

Beau felt himself chomping at the bit, but he realized it would be a wasted effort to storm a bowling alley if it turned out Sam was being held in one of those thugs' homes. The thought turned his stomach.

# Chapter 37

Samantha felt, rather than saw, the vast size of the space she was in. Machinery hummed in the background, something like a furnace she guessed. The voices of the men faded away and then a door closed with finality.

They'd tugged at her arms, dragging her from the vehicle and into this enclosure, shoving her against a wall, and fastening her bound wrists to it. Now that they were gone, she eased her head toward her hands and flung away the dark cloth that had covered her face.

Deep gulps of air refreshed her, somewhat.

She took stock of her surroundings. She sat on a concrete floor, facing a concrete wall. Her hip was beginning to throb already from landing here. Dim light came from somewhere behind her.

Her wrists were still bound with rope, a scratchy sort

of twine, and she realized the men had clipped a short chain from the rope to a heavy metal loop mounted in the wall. The clip was a sort of carabiner—easy to operate when one could reach it with one's fingers. Not so easy in her situation.

She twisted so her back faced the wall, her arms awkwardly stretched over her left shoulder. It would be too painful to hold the position for long, but she did get a glimpse of the machinery across the room. Some kind of HVAC system, probably providing heat to the building with natural gas, too far away and too sleek to count on finding a rough edge to cut through her bindings.

She turned back to allow her right shoulder to lean against the wall. Obviously, her captors had not made a plan in advance to bring her here and hold her for a long time. They would have surely come up with some type of bedding or padded surface for her to sit on, and would have definitely come up with a better means of keeping her fixed to the wall than a simple carabiner.

The door, she noticed, had a simple twist-handle type of lock, no deadbolt. If she could make it over there, she could conceivably lock them out, although she realized they would have a key. She sighed, knowing she was too tired to think this through right now.

She settled against the wall and closed her eyes. She needed to rest and gather her strength. As she began to doze, she remembered something that had been nagging at her. At least two of the voices were vaguely familiar to her. If she could only remember where she'd heard them before.

The furnace continued to shut down and come back on at regular intervals, lulling her to relax. Until she heard the doorknob turn and footsteps enter the room. Her eyes flew open.

"Shit!" yelled the man as he crossed the open space. He snatched up the cloth bag she'd tossed aside and jammed it down over her head again, this time cinching a cord around the top of it, digging it into her neck.

Now she remembered.

# Chapter 38

Beau ran his hands over the stubble on his chin, staring at the front of the bowling alley from a parking lot across the street and a half-block away, realizing how many hours he'd been awake. He wanted to sneak over there, to break in if necessary, to find out once and for all if Sam was inside.

But he couldn't see the back or the east side of the building, couldn't know if the kidnappers were around. He gave himself a little lecture. He had to be at his best now— no matter how long this took. He pictured the security team at Sterling, methodically searching that huge facility. No help would be coming from their direction anytime soon.

Aiden had said the highway patrol would spread out to storm the residences of all three suspects. Protocol would dictate that they execute a coordinated effort, doing their best to arrive at all three locations at once, so none of the suspects could alert the others. Searching a residence shouldn't take long, and if Aiden got word to them, perhaps Beau could expect reinforcements from that sector.

And what about from the kidnappers' point of view? There had been no demands yet. What was that about? He leaned his head against the back of his seat, considering. In the previous disappearances, it seemed a Sterling employee had been nabbed, held for a while, and instructed to quit the job and move out of town. Was this something similar? Was this intended as a warning for him to give up on the case and leave?

He jumped when his phone alerted him to an incoming text message. It was from Aiden: **All clear at Glasser residence**.

Four minutes later, another ping: **Clear at Emerson place too**.

That left Joe Sparling's home. The police officer would be armed. Beau hoped Sam wasn't there. Somehow, he had a feeling.

Impatient, he dialed Aiden's number. "I've got eyes on the bowling alley," he said.

"Beau, are you—"

"I'm just watching. No sign of movement, but I can't see the back without the risk of being spotted."

"I'm on my way. And Chief Redmond with State says he'll dispatch the others to that location next. We just got word that no one was at Sparling's residence either."

Beau told Aiden where to find him. As soon as he ended that call, he texted Carson Delaney. The quick response told him they'd not found Sam at the Sterling location, at least not yet.

**Hal Emerson and Ronnie Glasser scanned in for work this morning.** Carson's message didn't do a lot to answer Beau's questions.

Joe Sparling was still an unknown. He was debating about calling the Creston PD and casually asking for the officer when Aiden's SUV pulled into the parking lot beside him. He got out and walked around to the back, where he pulled out a sleek plastic case.

"I always hated surveillance," he told Beau, "but this little beauty almost makes it fun."

Beau watched, impressed, as Aiden opened the case and pulled out a small drone, no more than eight inches across. He set it aside and got out the controller, tested everything quickly, and launched it into the air. The little aircraft took off for the bowling alley.

Aiden shifted position so Beau could watch the screen and see the images the little guy was sending back. Within two minutes, they knew what they needed to know and Aiden directed the drone back to him.

A shiny black Oklahoma Highway Patrol car pulled in behind Beau's truck. Two officers emerged. Beau and Aiden stepped forward to confer with them. "We'll have another ten men on site soon," one of them told Aiden, who in turn introduced Beau as the sheriff of Taos County. Beau decided to let that stand. He needed all the authority he could get at this moment.

"Your wife is the one they've taken?"

"She is. She's smart and savvy, and she's been deputized by my department on more than one occasion. But we think this is three men against one woman, and I have to say, I want her out of there ASAP."

"Right." The younger officer gave him a skeptical look. "I don't know if our commander would want—"

"Listen, I know this isn't by the book," Beau started, locking eyes with each of them to convey the gravity of the situation. "But we're law enforcement, not lone wolves. It's our duty to ensure justice is served—and served safely." He paused, letting the words sink in. "Sam's life might be at stake, but so are ours."

That seemed to put the others somewhat at ease, and when several more patrol cars rolled up, the word spread that Beau would lead the way.

"Aiden, share your findings please," he said with a nod toward the drone sitting in the back of the PI's vehicle.

"We've spotted two vehicles behind the building, a sedan and a black Tahoe. That means a minimum of two guards."

"Probably just the two," Beau added. "The Tahoe belongs to Jason Blackwood. I don't know about the sedan." He filled them in on what Carson Delaney had told him, that the other two suspects had logged in at work.

"We find Sam, we get her out, and then we deal with Blackwood and his goons."

Nods all around. He assured himself that the teams were equipped with battering rams and everyone was armed, even while he hoped it wouldn't come down to a shootout. He assigned four of the patrol cars to encircle the bowling alley, two approaching from each side. He and Aiden would take the front. The PI held up his set of lock picks.

"Let's move."

The small armada of cars began to roll out, each of them taking their positions as a well-trained team. Beau and Aiden brought their vehicles to a stop at the front of the business, jumped out, and approached the door. Beau drew his pistol while Aiden aimed his lock picks at the deadbolt.

From the back of the building they could hear shouts. "Police! Open up!"

"Quick!" Aiden whispered to Beau. "We're in!"

They slipped through, into the lobby where customers would normally pay their fees, rent shoes, or whatever. The place felt hollow and silent without the usual clatter of pins and equipment, shouts and conversations of the bowlers. They glanced around until Beau spotted an Employees Only door to the left. He pointed and motioned Aiden forward.

Through the doorway, they found themselves in a hallway leading toward the rear of the building. Hitting light switches as they went, they ran past an employee locker room and a supply closet. A door marked Maintenance led to the pin-setting equipment that ran the full width of the alley. Beyond that was a door marked HVAC. Beau reached for the doorknob; a pop from the back of the building told him what he needed to know.

Pistols ready, he mimed for Aiden to keep watch on the long hallway as he stepped inside. What he saw froze him in place.

Smooth as a snake, Jason Blackwood emerged from the darkness, his slicked-back hair in place, the very picture of smug control. He grabbed Sam roughly, pulling her in front of him, a human shield. Her hands were bound but Beau could tell she'd been working at the frayed pieces of rope.

"Ah, Beau," Jason cooed, his voice dripping with

disdain. "So predictable."

Beau's pulse quickened, but his face remained impassive, betraying none of the anger boiling inside him. Years of training molded his posture into one of relaxed readiness. He took in the sight before him: Sam, resilient even in captivity, and Blackwood, the embodiment of arrogance.

"Jason," Beau acknowledged with a nod, his voice void of emotion yet laced with an undercurrent of steel.

Blackwood's lip curled into a sneer, his gaze sharp. Beau kept his eyes firmly on the other man, but his senses took in more. A shuffle behind a crate, a shadow flitting across the wall—his team was in position.

"Let her go, Jason," Beau said, the words almost casual. "You don't have to do this."

"Come now, Cardwell," Blackwood taunted. "We both know that's not how this ends. You just couldn't stop pushing, could you?"

Beau shifted slightly, a signal only a seasoned eye would catch.

"Answers, Jason," Beau demanded. "Now."

"Me, answering to you?" Blackwood's laugh echoed off the high ceilings, cold and hollow. "How quaint."

With Jason's attention diverted, Sam's fingers worked frantically at her bindings. The rough twine had chafed against her skin, but Beau could see her determination.

"Talk all you want, Beau. You'll get nothing from me," Jason smirked, mistaking Beau's silence for compliance.

Beau's eyes were steady—calculating. Sam sent a triumphant smile toward him as her wrists slipped free. They exchanged a look, and Beau gave the signal to the rest of the team.

Sam jammed an elbow into Blackwood's gut, her other

forearm catching him in the throat and he doubled over. His eyes widened a fraction as Beau came at him, his body a blur of motion.

Four SWAT officers rushed forward, weapons aimed. Jason Blackwood crumpled.

Beau pulled Sam out of the way, crushing her to his chest. Over her head he could see Aiden, leading Joe Sparling into the room, holding him at gunpoint.

# Chapter 39

Sam rubbed ointment into the raw skin on her wrists and thanked the female officer for thinking to provide it. They were at the Highway Patrol station in Enid, and she actually had no idea how many hours had passed since Beau, Aiden, and the SWAT team had come to her rescue. Although she figured she had a good chance of escaping anyway as soon as she got the ropes off and slugged Jason, she had to admit she'd never been as happy to see anyone as when Beau's handsome face appeared in that huge, gloomy room.

"They're ready to begin the interrogations now," the officer said. "Would you like to watch?"

Beau took Sam's elbow and walked her to a room where Aiden waited; they could monitor what was going on behind a mirrored wall. Beau, it seemed, would be one of the interrogators since he'd been far more involved in the investigation than any of the state troopers.

"They've got Jason in one room and Joe Sparling in another," Aiden told her. "Joe's the weaker link. He's already claiming the whole scheme was Jason's idea and he went along with nabbing you because he was ordered to."

"That sounds about right. I listened to voices, even when they had covered my head. I heard three men, and I'm pretty sure Jason was not one of them. He showed up later, at the bowling alley. At the time, I only saw the furnace room."

Aiden nodded. They turned their attention to the scenario before them. Behind the glass, Jason sat in a small room dominated by a metal table that was bolted to the floor. His white shirt was grimy with dirt from the back room of the bowling alley, and his normally smoothed-back hair hung over his forehead.

Beau led with the softer questions. "We've located several people who 'disappeared' in Creston over the past couple of years. They've said they were intimidated into quitting their jobs at Sterling and leaving town. What do you know about that?"

A casual shrug. "Nothing. Should I?"

"I'm thinking that's a yes. Joe Sparling has already caved. He says you're the one who ordered the abductions. Hal Emerson and Ronnie Glasser have been picked up and are being brought here. My wife will identify all of them. And you most certainly were there, holding Sam hostage, when I arrived this morning."

Another shrug. Sam felt her temper rise. "I'd like another chance at his ribcage, if I could."

Aiden chuckled.

"We have evidence, gathered by Mark Mitchell, that

chips were being diverted off the production and secretly shipped to the Chinese."

"Pfft! Nonsense."

"Is it? Jay Cormorant doesn't seem to think so. Johnny Smith has already talked to us."

At the mention of the two names that could definitely condemn him, Jason visibly paled. "Look, we never shipped any viable chips out of the country. Anything that went to China was just junk."

"Over and over again, for years, they continued to pay for junk? I seriously doubt that, but I'm sure we can find receivers on the other end who will let us know."

"Everything I did, I did for Olivia."

"You mean, at her request?"

"I mean, I wanted to build the reputation of the company, to increase revenues, to expand our customer base, to impress her. She and I, we're getting married and together we'll make Blackwood-Sterling the biggest and best in microchips—more successful than Intel or Nvidia."

Beau considered the things Olivia had told him. This man was delusional, in every way. "Sounds like mighty big plans. Of course, we have Olivia on her way here, and I'm sure she'll confirm it all."

Jason slumped a little further in his seat.

"Just one other little question remains—somewhat different subject." Beau had the man's attention. "Who actually knifed Mark Mitchell? Was that you or one of your henchmen?"

"What! NO!" Jason was upright in the chair now, his eyes searching the faces of the lawmen. "A little intimidation … maybe. It's all I wanted to accomplish with our little visit with your wife, just get you guys to leave town. But killing—no."

Beau came at it from a different angle. Of course, the guy wasn't going to flat-out admit it. "Mark knew his killer, allowed the person to get in close to him. That's a fairly limited number of people. You being one of them."

"I tell you, man. Not me, not my guys." His hand was shaky as he pushed the errant hair off his forehead. "I'll take a lie detector test, whatever you want. I never killed anyone."

Beau's skepticism showed. He gave one of the state troopers the chance to take over, but the answers were the same.

Finally, Jason drew the line. "I think I want a lawyer now."

Beau left the suspect and walked into the room where Sam and Aiden were observing the questioning. "What do you think?"

"I'm tired and probably not thinking straight," Sam said, "but he seems convincing."

Aiden nodded. "Same here. But, if there's one thing I learned as an MP, it's not to believe anything from a guy in this situation. He's got nothing to lose and everything to gain if he can get you to believe him."

Beau swore silently. "Yeah. We need forensic evidence. I'm hoping these guys from state can get hold of what Rollie Benson has been withholding from us."

"It's about all we can do for now," Aiden agreed.

"Let's just say … what if Jason is telling the truth? Then what? Who did kill Mark?"

Aiden slowly shook his head. "If not Jason, it's gotta be someone in his circle. We'll just have to dig deeper."

Sam caught Beau's eye. Neither of them wanted to

stay on in Creston another day, much less the amount of time this could take. They excused themselves, while Aiden turned his attention to the other interrogation room, where one of Jason's thugs, Hal Emerson, sat at the table like a chunk of belligerent muscle.

The hallway bustled with activity, office staff and troopers all seeming to be on the way somewhere. As they emerged into the waiting area in the lobby, they spotted Olivia Sterling in her usual work attire, a crisp skirt suit. Her normally precise bun seemed a little frazzled today.

"Come to retrieve Jason?" Sam asked.

"Hardly." Her mouth turned downward. "I can't believe how I put so much trust in him. I thought Jason and I were a team, taking the company to greater heights, as they say."

"For what it's worth, that's essentially what he said, too, during the questioning. With the addition that he pictured the company name becoming Blackwood-Sterling."

Olivia rolled her eyes. "Somehow, that part doesn't surprise me." She gave a deep sigh. "I should have known something was up when our profits took a dive. You can't sell at deep discounts forever, which is what I suspect he was doing with what he shipped to China. Not to mention, at least one of the businesses over there bought our chips for the sole purpose of replicating them and flooding the market. It's going to be a long haul for Sterling Microchips to recover from this."

"Are you here to talk with the police?" Sam asked, feeling more sympathetic to Olivia's situation.

"Eventually. But my first order of business is to fire Jason and the others who were involved with what happened to you, Sam." She held out a hand to each of them. "And I'm glad I ran into you because I can't thank you enough for being here and for pursuing this. I put too much faith in the Creston police, having no idea how deeply Rollie Benson has been under Jason's control. It's what I get for being in too many places at once, not paying enough attention to details."

"But how could you know?" Sam squeezed her hand. "You thought your trust was well placed."

"That's coming to an end as soon as I meet with the Chief of Patrol in about five minutes. I have a feeling the entire Creston department is in for a big shakeup." Olivia heard someone call her name and she turned to take that meeting.

"I'm so tired I could sleep for a week," Sam told Beau as they walked out to his pickup truck.

He put an arm around her shoulders. "I know. Me too. Let's get home."

He meant Cecelia's house. Sam thought wistfully of their comfy ranch house with the log walls and their two dogs waiting for them, a fire in the big stone fireplace, and the scent of a fresh pumpkin pie from Sweet's Sweets.

That little dream-bubble popped when they pulled up at Cece's and saw another car in the driveway. So much for an immediate nap.

# Chapter 40

Cecelia saw them coming and practically flew out the door to embrace Sam. "Oh my Lord, we were worried. I'm so thankful you're okay."

"Who's here?" Beau asked as they walked up the front steps.

"Oh. Ethan. He stopped by to see how I was doing. Of course I'd already got your call, so now we're just sitting here visiting. You must be hungry. Let me make you some breakfast, or lunch, or whatever you want. You just name it."

"Actually, I—" Sam didn't get the words out before they were in the foyer.

Ethan rose from one of the living room sofas and crossed the room to shake Beau's hand. "So, it was Jason Blackwood all along, huh?"

Cece interrupted again, declaring she would have eggs, bacon, sausages, and pancakes on the table in fifteen minutes. "Ethan, you'll stay too?"

Sam excused herself to freshen up, wishing instead that she could beg off and simply fall into bed. But that would be rude. Everyone had questions and, face it, she would probably lie there and her mind would begin churning anyway.

Their room had been tidied, the bed made, and fresh towels laid out in the bathroom. She pulled out some clean clothes and stepped into the shower, ready for the hot water to revive her energy long enough to get through a big breakfast. When she came out, she spotted the carved box on top of the dresser. This would do it.

She pulled on the fresh slacks and top, ran her fingers through her hair, and picked up the ancient artifact. The dull wood began to turn golden brown, the inlaid stones glowing as it warmed to her touch. Her chafed wrists had been stinging but now the redness subsided.

"Okay, enough of this or I'll never catch that nap." She set the box down and followed the scent of bacon that was wafting up from the kitchen.

Cecelia had the table set for four. She was stirring a big skillet of scrambled eggs, while Ethan stood beside her at the stove, flipping pancakes.

"Y'all sit," Cece insisted. "There's coffee in that metal carafe. I just made it while you were upstairs."

"I'm about coffee'd out," Sam said. "Is there still some of the orange juice that was in the fridge a couple days ago?"

She headed that way, slipping past the pair at the stove. Ethan picked up a full platter of pancakes and turned in her direction, meeting her gaze. A dark red aura surrounded his head and shoulders.

Startled, Sam backed up, bumping into Cece. "Oh, sorry!" When she looked back at Ethan, the aura had faded to a dull orange.

*What was that?*

She pulled out the carton of juice and helped herself to a glass from the cupboard. "Anyone else?" No takers, so she poured her own and went back to the table. When she looked at Ethan again, his aura had vanished.

She helped herself to the food, suddenly realizing she had an appetite. As she cut into the sausage links, she mulled over the curious aura. In the past she'd seen auras around people, and they either turned out to be perfectly benign or the intensity of the aura pointed her toward a guilty suspect.

"Okay, Beau, you promised to update me when you got home, so spill it." Cece picked up a wedge of her pancake.

Beau kept it to the minimum, leaving out the drama of the capture and Sam's ordeal. "It seems Jason Blackwood had worked his way into Jay Cormorant's trust and got names of Jay's relatives in China, an inroad into smuggling computer chips out of Sterling Microchip and into the hands of their leading overseas competitors. When Jay found out, he shut down his own business and moved away. But Jason had established a team over at Sterling, including a couple of men on the assembly line."

"What happened to all those people who went missing in recent years?" Ethan asked.

"As far as Aiden has learned, the kidnappings were done to intimidate Sterling employees into keeping their mouths shut and leaving town. A few resisted—those jobs at Sterling paid very well, but eventually the pressure mounted and they all left."

Cecelia set her fork down. "Is that what they were doing to Mark? Intimidating him to quit and move away?"

Beau shook his head. "Mark may have been a somewhat different case. For one thing, he knew more, had dug further into the records and documented his findings."

"But to kill him?" Her voice cracked. "I would have agreed to leave town in a minute if I'd known what was going on."

Beside her, Ethan placed an arm around her shoulders. Cece sat a little straighter. Sam felt a buzzing in her ears and watched them. Ethan's aura was back—orange now.

What was going on here? Did Cece and Ethan have a thing going?

He gave a quick squeeze and went back to his meal. He poured more syrup on his last pancake and casually faced Beau. "What do the police think—was Jason the one responsible for Mark?"

"We don't know. Jason swears he didn't kill him, doesn't know who did. He's pretty adamant, even agreed to do a lie detector test on that subject."

"Huh. I wouldn't believe a word that man says." Ethan stabbed the pancake, forking the final bite into his mouth.

"We'll see. Sometimes it takes a while for the whole truth to come out," Beau said. He pushed his empty plate aside.

Sam nudged his leg under the table. "Well, guys, I'm feeling the early morning hours. Let me help with the dishes and then I'm going to need a nap."

"Sam, no need to get the dishes at all. I'll put them in the dishwasher later," Cece insisted.

Sam picked up her plate and Beau's and carried them

to the sink, running hot water over the sticky surfaces.

"Well, this has been cozy," Beau said. "Thanks for the breakfast."

"Ethan was a big help," Cece said.

Sam glanced toward them at that moment. And that's when she knew.

# Chapter 41

The next two minutes felt surreal. From the moment she saw Ethan's devoted expression as he turned toward Cecelia, to the instant when Beau figured out that the librarian's high school crush was still very much alive and well, Sam saw the pieces click into place.

"Ethan," he said, standing, "maybe while the ladies see to the dishes, you and I can talk in the other room for a minute."

Ethan's dark eyes became sharp. He stood so suddenly that his chair tipped backward and he spun toward the kitchen island, where a wooden block of knives stood. Quicker than it took Sam to process his movements, he'd grabbed the longest knife from the block. Beau had already started toward the living room when Ethan charged after him.

"Beau! Look out!" she screamed.

She didn't see what happened next in the foyer, but heard the clatter of the knife on the marble floor. She ran toward the sound, shoving Cece away from the melee.

By the time she rounded the corner, Beau had Ethan in a chokehold. "Kick the knife out of the way, Sam, then get those handcuffs we used in Enid."

She did as instructed, locating the cuffs in the pocket of the coat he'd left in the living room.

"Ethan Hawthorne, I'm holding you on suspicion for the murder of Mark Mitchell." He automatically started to recite the Miranda warning as he clipped the handcuffs in place, even though he couldn't actually make an arrest.

Cece came out of the kitchen, her eyes wide with shock and dismay. "Ethan … what …?"

"I love you, Cece. I've always loved you." He broke down in sobs, his unruly hair standing out wildly by this time, his glasses lying on the floor.

The red aura, which had come back vividly as Ethan held the knife, vanished now in an instant, like a balloon that had popped. Sam stared at the air around him. Beau was talking and she had to pull her attention back to his words.

"Call the state Chief of Patrol. His card is in my coat pocket. I don't trust the Creston PD to handle this."

Sam found the card and made the call.

Ethan, meanwhile, continued to blubber on, talking to Cece. "I knew from Mark's research that he was about to blow something wide open at Sterling. After what happened to everyone else out there who threatened to expose Jason Blackwood, I knew it was just a matter of time before they'd threaten him and he would want to move away. And he would take you out of my life forever."

"Ethan, listen to yourself. I've never been *in* your life. Not really. We went to one middle school dance together. We've been friends, Ethan, but that was it."

"You served on the library board so you could spend time with me. We had a real connection." Tears ran down his face, and Sam nearly felt sorry for him.

"I served on the library board so our little town would have a library."

"We were on the hospital board together for a time."

"Same reason. Ethan, you have to believe me. There was never a romance here."

He crumpled to the floor with the sudden realization that he'd killed a man for a prize that was never going to be his.

# Chapter 42

"Can you stay in town at least through the arraignment?" Cecelia asked Beau, that night.

The three of them had settled into full-on comfort mode—pajamas and slippers, cashmere throws across their laps, bowls of popcorn between them, and a travel documentary about Scotland on the TV.

"Sure," Sam said. "Jason and his goons are in front of the judge tomorrow to enter their pleas. And Ethan's will follow."

Cece shook her head. "I still can't believe what Ethan said. Or what he did. I mean, he always seemed to be in sort of a different world, but I thought it was kind of cute, some kind of dreamy, literary … can I say hippie-dippy? I know that's not exactly a correct term."

"If it's any consolation, I never spotted anything close to a violent streak in him either," Sam said. Until that red aura. She hadn't mentioned it and never would. If Ethan had succeeded in catching up to Beau … if he'd harmed him, she could never live with it.

She glanced over at her handsome husband, who'd been oddly quiet since the troopers had hauled Ethan away. "Beau? What's up?"

He let out a long sigh. "Such a rookie mistake on my part, believing both crimes were perpetrated by the same person. Just because Sterling Enterprises was at the center of Mark's life and at the center of Jason's embezzlement, it doesn't follow that Jason killed Mark."

"But we all thought that," Cece argued.

He shook his head. "It's like the age-old scientific argument: Mary likes purple; teenagers like purple; therefore, Mary must be a teenager. Not necessarily so. I should have kept my thinking open to all the possibilities."

Sam and Cece both sent him encouraging smiles before Cece spoke up. "I'll tell you, I'm not at all happy with Rollie Benson for his shoddy police work. He ignored vital facts and should have come up with all the same things you discovered, Beau."

Anyone else would have preened a little at the compliment, but Beau explained. "With Rollie it was all about the money. Jason was paying him handsomely to look the other way, so of course he wasn't going to dig deeply into a murder case that most likely would expose his benefactor. Aiden was there when the state patrol guys called Benson in on the carpet. He told me Rollie did nothing but whine about how little he's paid in his job."

Sam squeezed his hand. "Yours didn't pay a fortune either, but it didn't cause you to become a criminal yourself."

"It's weird but I miss the life," Beau said, his gaze faraway.

* * *

The Garfield County courthouse was buzzing when they arrived. News channels had picked up on the story, and crews from as far away as Oklahoma City were standing around their vans, satellite dishes aimed toward the sky. Reporters checked hair and makeup in handheld mirrors and murmured to their cameramen until cars began rolling to the curb in front of the courthouse in Enid.

A few reporters rushed Olivia Sterling when she stepped out of a limo that was probably hired by her attorneys. They coached her to say nothing more inflammatory than "justice will prevail" before turning their backs and walking up the steps.

Jason Blackwood also arrived by limo, flanked by a legal team that would have made OJ Simpson proud. His two goons, Emerson and Glasser, were apparently now on their own, each arriving with one lawyer.

Sam, Beau, and Cecelia kept to the fringe of the crowd, and as soon as Aiden arrived, they edged their way inside, went through the security checkpoint, and found seats in the crowded courtroom. It seemed half the population of Creston was there, probably because most were employed at Sterling and had a vested interest in what would happen.

The judge, a no-nonsense black woman, banged her gavel and read the charges against Jason. When she came to 'abduction, grand theft, and embezzlement,' it seemed she took extra pleasure in making the words sound serious. No, Sam thought, those charges *are* serious. She hoped a jury would see through the slick businessman and dole out a sentence appropriate to the misery he had caused and the huge amount of money he had taken.

Jason, of course, pleaded not-guilty. The judge denied two petitions by his attorneys to drop the charges, and he was bound over for trial—free on the conditions that he turn in his passport, wear a tracking band on his ankle, and not leave the county. If he violated any of those terms, she made it clear he would be locked up until his trial and that he would not like jail. Sam noticed Olivia Sterling smiled at that.

With a few more bangs of the gavel, his cohorts received the same treatment.

Then it was Ethan's turn. He'd not been able to come up with bail sufficient to cover a murder charge, so he'd been remanded to the county jail for the past two days. He looked definitely worse for the wear, walking into the courtroom in an orange jumpsuit.

Cece made a small sound in her throat at the sight of him. Sam couldn't tell whether it was sympathy for his condition or fury at seeing him again, knowing he'd made her a widow. She suspected the latter.

When asked for his plea, Ethan stood up and uttered the word: Guilty. His lawyer seemed resigned; he must have tried to dissuade him from that choice.

Sam felt a wave of sadness. She had genuinely liked Ethan when they met him. But she also understood the strain of keeping such a secret and that it would have taken a toll on him already. Remaining in a county jail for months and then facing a trial, when there were witnesses who'd heard him confess ... No, she could understand why he just wanted to get it over with.

The judge questioned whether he was aware that this would mean the rest of his life spent behind bars in a state prison. Or worse. The death penalty was also a possibility. He nodded, resigned. A murmur went through the courtroom, but their small group sat in stunned silence.

It was over.

# Author's Note

Dear Reader, I started to write an epilogue to this story, in which Beau and Sam say goodbye to Cece and return home to Taos to resume their normal lives. There is the upcoming Thanksgiving holiday, which will have Sam busy at the bakery, and there are some unexpected events in the lives of the other characters in the series …

Well, before I knew it the epilogue had turned into multiple chapters and those chapters have morphed into something even longer. So I'm going to leave you with this little teaser and the promise that Samantha and Beau's Thanksgiving this year will be eventful, and it will be presented to you as the next book in the series. Or perhaps a novella this fall, because with the holidays coming up, who has time to read something longer? Watch for *Thankful Sweets*, coming soon!

Thank you for taking the time to read *Secret Sweets*.
If you enjoyed it, please consider telling your friends or
posting a short review. Word of mouth is an author's best
friend and is much appreciated.
Thank you,
Connie Shelton

\* \* \*

**Get another Connie Shelton book—FREE!**
**Visit her website at connieshelton.com**
**or scan the QR code to find out how!**

**Sign up for Connie Shelton's free mystery**
**newsletter at www.connieshelton.com**
**and receive advance information about new**
**books, along with a chance at prizes, discounts and**
**other mystery news!**

**Contact by email: connie@connieshelton.com**
**Follow Connie Shelton on Twitter, Pinterest,**
**Instagram and Facebook**

## Books by Connie Shelton

## The Charlie Parker Series
*Deadly Gamble*
*Vacations Can Be Murder*
*Partnerships Can Be Murder*
*Small Towns Can Be Murder*
*Memories Can Be Murder*
*Honeymoons Can Be Murder*
*Reunions Can Be Murder*
*Competition Can Be Murder*
*Balloons Can Be Murder*
*Obsessions Can Be Murder*
*Gossip Can Be Murder*
*Stardom Can Be Murder*
*Phantoms Can Be Murder*
*Buried Secrets Can Be Murder*
*Legends Can Be Murder*
*Weddings Can Be Murder*
*Alibis Can Be Murder*
*Escapes Can Be Murder*
*Old Bones Can Be Murder*
*Sweethearts Can Be Murder*
*Money Can Be Murder*
*Road Trips Can Be Murder*
*Cruises Can Be Murder*
*Holidays Can Be Murder - a Christmas novella*

Connie Shelton is the *USA Today* bestselling author of more than 50 novels and several non-fiction books. She taught writing classes for six years and was a contributor to *Chicken Soup For the Writer's Soul*. She and her husband currently live in northern New Mexico.

Visit her website to learn more!

Made in United States
Orlando, FL
16 July 2024

49029735R00171